Anonymous

Lives of Missionaries, Greenland

Hans Egede; Matthew Stach and his associates

Anonymous

Lives of Missionaries, Greenland
Hans Egede; Matthew Stach and his associates

ISBN/EAN: 9783337316914

Printed in Europe, USA, Canada, Australia, Japan

Cover: Foto ©Raphael Reischuk / pixelio.de

More available books at **www.hansebooks.com**

NEW HERRNHUT.

FACE 181.

LIVES OF MISSIONARIES.

———◆✕◆———

GREENLAND.

———

HANS EGEDE.

MATTHEW STACH,

AND HIS ASSOCIATES.

———◆◇◆———

PUBLISHED UNDER THE DIRECTION OF
THE COMMITTEE OF GENERAL LITERATURE AND EDUCATION,
APPOINTED BY THE SOCIETY FOR PROMOTING
CHRISTIAN KNOWLEDGE.

———◆◇◆———

LONDON.

SOCIETY FOR PROMOTING CHRISTIAN KNOWLEDGE,

NORTHUMBERLAND AVENUE, CHARING CROSS;

43, QUEEN VICTORIA STREET; AND 48, PICCADILLY.

———

NEW YORK: POTT, YOUNG, & CO.

MEMOIR OF HANS EGEDE,

THE NORWEGIAN MISSIONARY IN GREENLAND.
1686—1758.

" One man soweth, and another reapeth."

AMONGST the servants of Christ to whom it has
been appointed to sow the seed but not to reap
the harvest, few perhaps, in modern times, have
had their faith and hope so severely tried as
Hans Egede, the father of Greenland Missions.

Hans (or *John*) Egede was born in Norway,
in the year 1686. The simple, hardy habits
which characterize the domestic life of the Norwegians early accustom the young to join in
the occupations and sports of their elders, both
on land and water. But the toils and pastimes
in which Egede was allowed to participate did
not lessen his fondness for reading : he was eager
to acquire knowledge, and the long winter nights
of the north afforded him abundant leisure for the
pursuit of his favourite studies. His disposition
had ever been loving and hopeful, ready to help
and quick to sympathize ; and as his years ripened
into manhood, it was seen that the love of God

was the main-spring of his kindness to his neighbour, and the governing motive which was to
actuate his life. He had remembered his Creator
in the days of his youth, and heartily desired to
spend all his days in serving Him. At the age
of three-and-twenty he was appointed to the
charge of the parish of Vogen, in the north of
Norway; and it might well have seemed that
this was the place in which his best hopes and
aspirations were to receive their accomplishment.
He had before him a life of labour, but it was labour which he loved; he was the stay and comfort
of aged parents; and he had united himself to a
wife who was every way worthy of him. And in
spite of the anxieties and discouragements which
must sometimes sadden the heart of every faithful
pastor, Egede esteemed himself, and was esteemed
by his neighbours, a happy man. But God had
selected him for a post of greater trial and less
cheering labour.

It may be proper here to remind the reader
that, at the period to which this narrative refers,
the kingdoms of Denmark and Norway were united
under the government of the same sovereign.
The reigning king, Frederic IV., had, a few years
before, set an example of godly enterprise by
establishing a mission for the conversion of the
heathen at Tranquebar, in the East Indies. Some
tokens of success were already cheering the hearts
of the faithful men who had gone thither; and
the letters in which they narrated their proceed-

ings, and described the manner in which the Gospel was received by the idolatrous natives of the country, were read with lively interest by pious members of the Danish Church, and found their way also into the sister-kingdom of Norway. Nowhere, perhaps, did these records of missionary labour awaken more interest and sympathy than in the secluded parsonage of Vogen. Rejoicing much that Christ was preached to the heathen on that distant Indian shore, Egede began to inquire if there was no way by which the same blessed message might be carried to the benighted men of other lands.

The foreign dependencies of Denmark were few in number. Tranquebar in India, and some small islands in the West Indies, constituted the whole. In earlier ages, however, the men of Denmark and Norway had been amongst the most daring and successful of European adventurers and colonists. Spreading themselves east and west, north and south, they had conquered territories and king-doms, and had bequeathed to their descendants wealth and dominion in lands wider and more fruitful than their own.

But Egede remembered that there had been one little colony of Norwegians whose history presented a melancholy contrast to that of their more favoured brethren. In the days of the Sea-kings, and about the same time that our own king Alfred was obliged to retreat for a while before the swarms of Northmen who invaded England, a company of Norwegians, led by Earl Ingolf, had taken possession of Iceland (A.D. 874). From thence, a century afterwards, Eric the Red sailed out in quest of a new home, and discovered in the west an uninhabited country, which he called Greenland (982). A name which appears singularly inappropriate, since fields of ice, naked rocks, and snow-covered mountains are the most conspicuous objects which meet the eye of the mariner as his vessel nears the coast. Yet even on these ice-bound shores there are slopes and valleys lying beneath the shelter of the rocks, which the short arctic summer clothes with verdure. Birds innumerable build amongst the cliffs and islets, reindeer browse in the valleys, and herds of seals bask on the shore. It seemed a desirable land to Eric and to the companions whom he induced to share his fortunes. They established themselves on the west coast, gradually extending their settlements north and south as their numbers were increased by fresh colonists from Iceland and Norway.

Hitherto the inhabitants of these countries had been heathens; worshipping Thor and Odin, the gods of Scandinavia. But the Christian religion penetrated into Norway. The king, Olaus, ranged himself on the side of the believers, and being zealous for the extension of the faith which he had espoused, sent a Christian teacher to convert the Norwegians of Greenland. Eric listened, and declared himself a Christian, and most of the colonists followed his example. His sons, bold, adventurous navigators, trod in their father's steps, and sailed from Greenland still farther to the west, to find a new territory. They reached the shores of North America, and spent the greater part of two years in a well-wooded country, believed to have been a portion of what is now called Canada. The sons of Eric called it *Wineland*, because of the wild grapes which grew in the forest. Hitherto they had encountered none of their own kind; the birds of the air and the beasts of the wood appeared to be the only tenants of this goodly region. But in the third year, sailing farther to the north, they fell in with a diminutive dark-skinned people (evidently a tribe of Esquimaux), whom they called, in derision, *Skrœlings*, or *dwarfs*. These newly converted Northmen, though they had to a certain degree adopted the Christian religion, had learnt little or nothing of its lesson of peace and goodwill to all men. The scorn with which they beheld the Skrœlings did not restrain them from more active manifestations of enmity : they attacked and killed several in mere wantonness, and thus provoked a struggle with the whole tribe, in which the Norwegian leader was slain.

Notwithstanding this inauspicious commencement, however, emigrants from Greenland, Iceland, and Norway repaired to the newly discovered land, founded a settlement, and for a time prospered. Could they have lived in peace with

one another, the Wineland colonists might have
become the fathers in America of a nation of European origin, more than four centuries before the
great discoveries of Columbus. But they were a
fierce and quarrelsome race; and the progress of
the new settlement was soon arrested by discord
and bloodshed. Some of the survivors of these
broils remained in the country, but the colony was
dispersed, and Wineland ceased to be resorted to.
In the following century, indeed, a zealous missionary from Greenland undertook a voyage
thither, in the hope of finding out the descendants
of his countrymen, and converting them to Chris-
tianity. But it does not appear that his benevolent expedition was rewarded with any success.
The ancient discoveries of the Northmen gradually faded from recollection, and the fate of their
American brethren was never certainly known.
In this respect the history of Wineland was like
a foreshowing of the doom which some centuries
later awaited the Greenland Norwegians.

During four hundred and fifty years Greenland
maintained a regular, though infrequent, intercourse with Norway. A magistrate deputed by
the king administered the civil government of the
country; and a succession of bishops, appointed
by the Archbishop of Drontheim, presided over
the Greenland Church. It paid also its annual
tribute to the Pope; not in money, which was
very scarce in the colony, but in the ivory tusks
of the walrus. Like their countrymen in Norway,

the people were hunters, fishers, and herdsmen ; but, unlike their enterprising forefathers, they concerned themselves hardly at all with navigation, the difficulties of which appear indeed to have increased as years rolled on. Enormous icebergs, floating along the coast, and often filling the inlets, had been seen with wonder by the first discoverers of Greenland ; but now the ever-accumulating belt of ice which had formed along the shore entirely blocked up, during many months of the year, the entrance of the fiords on the shores of which the colonists dwelt. Years occasionally intervened between the arrival of vessels from Norway. Yet, infrequent as was the communication of Greenland with the more civilized portions of the world, its remoteness did not exempt it from the awful scourge of the Black Death which ravaged all Asia and Europe in the middle of the fourteenth century. This dreadful pestilence was especially fatal to the inhabitants of Northern Europe. Not only men, but cattle fell beneath its baneful influence ; and even the vegetable world is said to have been blasted by its breath. A year before the Black Death appeared in Greenland, the colony had been visited for the first time by a party of Skrœlings or Esquimaux. The Norwegians, proud, like their fathers, of their superior strength and stature, and forgetting that God hath made of one blood all nations of men to dwell on the earth, contemned their dwarfish visitors, and drove them away with insult. A skirmish ensued, in which the arrows of the feeble strangers proved fatal to several of their assailants. They retired, nevertheless, but returned in greater numbers some years afterwards, when the population of the colony, never very large, had been greatly thinned by the plague. Some of the most desirable valleys had lost all their inhabitants. Of these the new comers took possession, and gradually advanced upon the enfeebled Norwegians. The people of Norway had themselves suffered terribly from the plague. Absorbed in their own troubles, they ceased for some years to bestow any thought upon their brethren in Greenland. And when they renewed their intercourse with the colony, the times were not favourable. The crowns of Denmark, Sweden, and Norway had fallen (1397) to the same sovereign, Margaretta, " the Semiramis of the North." The cares of three kingdoms left her and her successors little leisure to attend to the concerns of that small remote possession. About the same time several vessels freighted for Greenland by the merchants of Bergen, were successively lost by storms. Utterly discouraged, they at length abandoned the trade altogether ; and a rumour grew that all the people in Greenland had been exterminated by a hostile fleet, coming no man knew from whence. But although this report was not generally credited, one hundred years passed away, and nothing more was done to relieve the unfortunate colonists.

Then Walkendorf, the Archbishop of Drontheim, moved with pity for their forlorn condition, projected the renewal of intercourse with Greenland; devised means of providing the people with pastors, sought out suitable persons to emigrate thither as colonists, and collected all the information that could be obtained for the guidance of the mariners who were to take part in the enterprise. Unhappily, Walkendorf fell into disgrace with his sovereign, and going into voluntary banishment, died in a foreign land, and his benevolent schemes perished with him (1521).

In the space of sixty years three kings in succession formed plans for the recovery of their lost colony, and even began to fit out ships and make preparations for the undertaking; yet none of these projects were carried into effect. In the meantime, the English navigator, John Davis, in the course of three voyages which he made to search for "a north-west passage to India and Cathaye" (1585-1587), repeatedly visited the west coast of Greenland, where, however, he saw only Esquimaux, who willingly came to barter skins of seals, reindeer, and white hares for such things as his men had to give them. From this time English vessels often touched on the Greenland coast, and their representations of the profits which might be obtained by trading ships stirred up the Danish sovereigns to make a fresh attempt for the re-discovery of their ancient settlements. King Christian II. engaged an English seaman,

experienced in the Greenland voyage, to pilot an
expedition which he sent out for that purpose.
The ships reached their destination safely, and
saw several spots which appeared pleasant and
fruitful, producing abundance of grass, brushwood,
and berries.   But the Danes alarmed and ex-
asperated the Esquimaux, by making some of
them prisoners, to carry them to Denmark; and
in their subsequent visits to the coast they found
the people resolute in rejecting all intercourse,
and prepared to repulse them if they attempted to
land.   Thus the object of the expedition was
frustrated. Voyages to Greenland were undertaken by several succeeding monarchs; but the
ice prevented some of the ships from reaching
the coast, and those which did so brought back
no satisfactory information.   At various times
the Danes brought away some of the Esquimaux;
but as no one understood their language, it was
impossible to obtain any information from them.
The fate of these poor people was most unhappy;
some pining themselves to death with grief at the
separation from their country and kindred, and
some escaping from captivity by throwing themselves into the sea.   By the time the seventeenth
century came to an end, the Danes had given up
their researches in despair; and very few even of
the Norwegians themselves remembered that a colony of their countrymen and fellow-Christians had
a home in Greenland in old times, and that some of
their descendants might even now be living there.

Egede, however, musing upon the subject, began to ask himself what could have become of those poor forsaken people. Moved, as he supposed, by mere curiosity, he wrote to a friend who had made several whaling voyages to Davis' Strait, and begged that he would tell him all that he knew about the present state of Greenland and its inhabitants. The answer of his correspondent led him to believe that the men of Norwegian descent, long abandoned by their countrymen, and left without Christian teachers, had sunk into paganism. Egede knew that even in Norway, where the word of God was openly read in every parish church, fragments of heathen superstitions, handed down from the old idolatrous times, still survived in the rural districts, and affected in some degree the minds of the people. In Greenland it could hardly be hoped that the light of truth had ever shone so clearly as it now did in the parent kingdom, for intercourse with the colony had ceased long before the reformation of religion, at a time when the Gospel of Christ was overlaid and obscured by human traditions and inventions. He pictured to himself the remnant of Christian Greenlanders, gradually losing the little light which their fathers had possessed, mingling with the heathen who had taken possession of their deserted dwelling-places, and becoming by degrees altogether like them, without any hope on which to stay themselves in life or death. Deep compassion for these forlorn people now took possession of his heart. It seemed to him the duty of every Norwegian to do something towards searching out his unhappy countrymen, and publishing to them the glad tidings of the Gospel; and his mind was constantly at work devising measures by which this charitable design might be accomplished. Soon the desire to be himself a messenger of salvation to those lost ones arose in his heart. But at this point many difficulties presented themselves. God had already given into his charge a flock to feed and tend; would it be right for him to abandon them? Moreover, he had not only a wife and infant child whom he dreaded to expose to the dangers of the seas, but an aged mother and other near relatives depended on him for sustenance; how would these be adequately provided for, if he were away? Perplexed by these thoughts, he endeavoured to drive Greenland quite out of his mind, or to remember it only in order to commit the objects of his compassionate concern to the pity and care of the Almighty.

This, however, he found to be impossible. Urged to proceed in the work by an inward impulse which grew stronger every day, yet withheld by attachment to his parish, by care for his family, and by the fear lest he should be thrusting himself upon a work for which he was not qualified, he had no rest in his spirit.

For many months his mental conflicts were known only to himself. To those around him he appeared occupied, as ever, in the duties of his parish, in study, or in the kindly offices which gladdened the daily life of those who depended upon him. Encouraged at length by the zeal with which king Frederic promoted the mission at Tranquebar, Egede, in the year 1710, ventured to direct the attention of his superiors to the long-forgotten Greenland colony, in the hope that some of his brethren in the ministry, more conveniently situated and better qualified than himself, might be willing to seek out these poor sheep wandering in a land of darkness. He addressed to the king a memorial, in which he humbly, but with much earnestness, urged the claims of the Norwegian Greenlanders to the compassionate consideration of their countrymen. But, sensible that the proposals of a young unfriended man like himself were little likely to receive much attention from the rulers of the state, he sent copies of his memorial to his diocesan, the Bishop of Drontheim, and to the Bishop of Bergen, the port which was chiefly concerned in the trade with the northern seas, accompanied by letters entreating them to use their influence to recommend the case of the Greenlanders to the favourable consideration of the sovereign and the council. In answer to this appeal the bishops, having taken time to deliberate on the subject, replied that they heartily approved of the object which Mr. Egede had in view, and would do their best to promote it; but they pointed out various obstacles which must at

c

present impede any attempt to commence a mission in Greenland. Egede himself had been aware of some of these, and in particular, that the war which the king of Denmark was then carrying on against Sweden might make it very difficult to provide money for any new missionary enterprise. But he hoped that this obstacle might soon be removed by the return of peace; and feeling that he had done all that was possible under present circumstances, his mind was at rest.

Soon, however, his tranquillity was disturbed by the expostulations, entreaties, and even reproaches of his own household. Hitherto he had said nothing to them on the subject in which he was so deeply interested. But his memorial, and the letters which he had addressed to the bishops, began to be talked about at Drontheim and Bergen. Some of his acquaintances who about this time visited the latter city, were amazed when they heard that their neighbour, the young minister of Vogen, had proposed a mission to Greenland, and was willing, if necessary, to take part in it himself. They reproached him vehemently with what they were pleased to call his foolhardiness, and setting before his wife and kindred, in the strongest light, all the privations, dangers, and distress which would attend their removal to a country so frigid and difficult of access, they urged them to interpose all their influence to prevent Mr. Egede from carrying into effect his preposterous scheme. Egede always looked back to this period of his life as one of peculiar suffering. He was a man of strong affections, and the tears and entreaties of his wife and mother almost overcame his resolution. For a little while, indeed, they did succeed in persuading him that he had been in error in supposing that it could be right for *him* to engage in such an undertaking. He even gave thanks to God for having delivered him from what he *now* believed had been a temptation of Satan, designed to divert his mind from the duties of his own charge. His family were greatly rejoiced at the change in his sentiments, and for a little while he was able to share their joy. But ere long the words of his Heavenly Master, " Whoso loveth father or mother more than Me is not worthy of Me," pierced his heart like a sword. His wife observed his deep distress, and strove to soothe him, but in vain. Neither the endearments of his home, nor the most diligent discharge of his pastoral duties, could afford him any comfort until he felt that he had surrendered his own will in this matter to the will of God. But his wife's distress caused him much sorrow. She could not bear to hear Greenland mentioned; and was unable to believe that it could ever be her duty to engage in a project which would separate her from her own mother and oblige her to expose her infant children to hardship and danger.

Until this time Egede and his family had enjoyed much outward peace and prosperity. They were now visited with a succession of troubles, the heaviest of which arose from the envy and ill-will of some persons from whom they might have hoped for better things. These trials and persecutions afflicted Mrs. Egede so deeply that she began to wish her husband might be removed to another parish. He exhorted her not to think so much of the mere outward causes and instruments of their troubles, but to regard them as the means by which God was weaning both her and himself from a home which they had loved too dearly, that they might become willing at His command to leave all, and go out into the wilderness. "He is saying to us, 'Arise and depart: this is not your rest.'" Following her husband's counsel, Mrs. Egede brought her sorrows, fears, and perplexities to God; and poured out her heart before Him in prayer. She received strength and comfort, and also the firm conviction that these trials were designed to animate her to a more resolute self-denial in the service of Christ. Henceforward, instead of opposing her husband's missionary plans, she encouraged him by her sympathy. He greatly needed it, for several years of delay and disappointment awaited him. He might almost have taken for his motto, "I have great heaviness and continual sorrow in my heart . . . . for my brethren, my kinsmen according to the flesh." But he stood alone. He had hoped that some clergyman of wisdom and experience would offer himself for the mission. Diffident of his own ability to fill an untried and difficult post, he desired to labour in

it under the direction of another, rather than to be
left entirely to his own discretion. But no one
appeared willing to engage in the work. A
numerous party in the kingdom objected even to
the maintenance of the mission in India, firmly
established as it already was, and distinguished
by marks of the Divine favour. The proposal to
establish a mission in Greenland was by almost
all men either ridiculed or condemned as impracticable.

In the year 1715, Egede published a small
treatise in which he examined the various objections alleged against his design, and proved their
futility by arguments drawn from reason and
Scripture. But if Egede's opponents were con-
futed, they were not silenced; and when they could
no longer raise a laugh at the folly of his schemes,
they were not ashamed to cast suspicion upon the
purity of his motives. Although they had previously reproached him with cruelty to his wife
and children, in proposing to exchange comfort
and competence at home for privation and danger
in a strange and savage land, they now accused
him of hiding a spirit of discontent under the cloak
of religion; and insinuated that his anxiety to establish a mission in Greenland sprang from a desire
to rise in the world, and not from any motives of
piety or benevolence. He, however, held patiently
on his way; fulfilling with diligence the duties
of his parish, but still pleading the cause of his
Greenland brethren at every fitting opportunity

by letters and memorials addressed to persons in
authority, and to the College of Missions, a council
which the king had established for the direction of
affairs relating to the Indian mission. But when
seven or eight years had passed away without
any advance being made, he perceived that he
must prosecute his design in person if he would
have it succeed. During the time which had
elapsed since the desire to be a missionary first
arose in his heart, his family circumstances had
undergone a sufficient change to make it possible
for him to give up his parish without injury to the
relatives who had depended on his assistance,
though not without impoverishing himself.

But he saw that this sacrifice was required of
him; and in the year 1718, with the consent of his
bishop, he resigned into other hands the parish
of Vogen. The final parting with his flock, and
with many dear friends and kindred who resided
amongst them, was a very sore trial. His solicitude
for the conversion of the Greenlanders had in no
degree lessened his attachment to the people of
his charge ; and when he was to preach to them for
the last time, and to bid them farewell, he was
almost overpowered with sorrow. Under God, his
wife was his support now. She resigned the comforts of home and the society of beloved friends
with such a cheerful serenity and acquiescence in
the Divine Will, that her husband was animated
by her example, and inspired with fresh strength
to persevere in his self-denying course.

One of the chief obstacles which might have prevented the King of Denmark from entering upon any new missionary enterprise, was at this time removed by the death of Charles XII. of Sweden, who perished by a random shot while besieging Fredericshall, in Norway: December 11th, 1718. It was foreseen that peace, on terms honourable and advantageous to Denmark, would now be concluded. Egede seized the favourable moment, repaired to Copenhagen, petitioned the College of Missions on behalf of Greenland, and had an audience of the king, who listened attentively to his statements, and dismissed him with the gracious assurance that he would consider the matter with care, and endeavour to find some means of maintaining the proposed mission.

Accordingly King Frederic devised a plan for settling colonists in Greenland, and establishing a regular intercourse between the colony and the mother-country, for which purpose a mercantile company was to be chartered. It appeared to him that this scheme might probably answer the double purpose of defraying the expense of the mission, and also of planting amongst the Greenlanders a civilized Christian community, from whose example they would learn some of the arts and refinements of life, at the same time that they were receiving from the missionaries the knowledge of the Gospel. And it was confidently hoped that by this means the ancient Norwegian settlements might not only be recovered, but restored to more than their former prosperity. A royal mandate was transmitted to the magistrates of Bergen, requiring them to examine the captains and pilots who had been engaged in the whale fishery on the coast of Greenland, in order to obtain all the information they could give for the guidance of settlers in that country. The king desired also that any persons willing to join in founding the new colony would consider what privileges they would desire to have assured to them, and promised to grant every reasonable request. Egede was full of hope now, but it was quickly disappointed. Not one of the seamen who were examined by the Bergen magistrates had a good word to say for Greenland. They all concurred in representing the voyage as so dangerous, and the country as so dreary, that the most sanguine adventurer could feel no inclination to become a colonist. Not long before, indeed, a report had reached Norway that the crew of a wrecked whaling vessel, who had escaped in a boat to the shore, had all been butchered and devoured by the savage inhabitants. And although this report was not altogether true, it was so in part; and being fully credited at the time, the horrors of cannibalism were added to the other uninviting circumstances of a residence in Greenland. Egede had one argument which to himself was a sufficient answer to every objection: "Our Lord has said, 'Go ye into all the world, and preach the Gospel to every creature. I am with you alway, even unto the end of the world.' If He be for us, who can be against us?" But this was not a consideration which had any weight with men who looked upon emigration to Greenland merely as a means of obtaining a comfortable maintenance. Egede, however, whose long consideration of the subject had led him, like the philanthropic archbishop Walkendorf, to seek for information of every kind concerning the country, knew that the merchants of other nations, the Dutch especially, derived considerable advantage from their trade with Greenland; and why should it not be equally profitable to his own countrymen? He failed not to press this question at every opportunity on the mercantile men to whom he could procure access; and though he met with many rebuffs and much ridicule at first, his indefatigable perseverance was at length rewarded with success. A few merchants were moved by his entreaties to venture something for the good of their country and the spread of the Gospel, and their example had its effect upon others. In the end it was determined to attempt a trading settlement in Greenland; and a company was formed, each member of which contributed £40 and upwards towards forming a capital. Mr. Egede himself gave £60 out of his small fortune; and the contributions of the bishop and clergy of the diocese raised the sum to £2000—a much larger amount in that age and country than a similar sum would be in our own.

With this money a ship was purchased, and

suitably equipped for conveying Mr. Egede **and**
his companions to Greenland. It was named the
' Hope.' A factor, or manager, was appointed to
conduct the trade; and several artisans and persons accustomed to rural occupations were selected
by the company to begin a settlement. Two
smaller vessels were to accompany the ' Hope;'
one for the whale-fishery, the other to return to
Norway with tidings of their arrival and welfare,
as soon as the settlers were fairly established on
Greenland ground. Before the arrangements were
quite completed, a joyful message arrived from the
College of Missions, stating that the king had signified his approval of the undertaking, and that he
appointed Mr. Egede Minister and Missionary in
the new colony, with a yearly salary of 60*l.*; he
had also given orders that 100*l.* should be presented to him immediately for the outfit of himself and his family.

Eleven years had elapsed since Egede began to
solicit the attention of his countrymen to the spiritual destitution of the Greenlanders. Many
times during those years he had almost said, " All
these things are against me!" and he tells us that
he was sorely tempted to murmur against God, who
had kindled in his heart an unquenchable desire to
preach the Gospel in Greenland, and yet defeated
every attempt which he made to carry the design
into effect. But he was full of joy and gratitude
now. On the 2nd of May, 1721, accompanied by
his wife and four young children, he went on board

the 'Hope,' and was presented to the seamen and emigrants (about forty in number) as the superintendent of the future colony. But the ships were not able to leave the harbour until ten days afterwards. On the 12th May they finally departed for their destination, and for the first eighteen days were favoured with tolerable weather. On the 4th June they passed Staatenhuk, the south-eastern extremity of Greenland, and indulged the hope that their voyage would soon be at an end. The weather however changed, and became exceedingly tempestuous, and the ships encountered enormous quantities of ice. The whaler had parted company with them at the beginning of the voyage, and they saw her no more. She had been overset in a squall, but having righted again, with the loss of her masts, had been driven on the coast of Norway : an inauspicious beginning of the mercantile operations of the company. The 'Hope' and her consort were beating about for three weeks, without drawing any nearer to their destination ; and the captain, despairing of a favourable termination to the voyage, had almost made up his mind to return to Bergen, when they descried an opening in the ice. But having ventured into it for some distance, they found that they could advance no farther. They would gladly have got back now to the open sea, but the wind was contrary, and blowing with great violence. The smaller vessel was driven on the ice, and sprang a leak ; and

both ships were in imminent danger of destruction
from the ice floes which drove violently against
them. To add to their distress, a thick fog sprung
up, and shrouded every object from view. In this

THE "HOPE" IN THE STORM.

extremity the captain of the 'Hope' bade his
passengers prepare for death, which he expected
every moment would overtake them. But they
looked unto God, and were lightened. Unseen by
them, His Providence was working out their de-
liverance by the storm which appeared to threaten
their destruction. It broke and dispersed the ice,

and when the veil of fog was lifted they found themselves, to their astonishment, in open water. Day by day the eyes of the emigrants were turned anxiously in the direction of their new country, but it was the 3rd July before they finally made the shore at Baal's River, in lat. 64° N. The coast reminded them in some degree of the land which they had left, but only the sternest features of Norwegian landscape were to be seen here; the numberless islets and rocks, the firths and inlets indenting all the shore, the majestic outlines of mountains in the background. But the snow, the glaciers, the bare sterile ruggedness of Greenland, told them that they were far indeed from their own magnificent coast, with its noble fiords, widening and narrowing in a thousand curves and channels—now enclosed between the mighty granite cliffs, now opening into lake-like expanses where the shores smiled with verdure, and the cheerful farmsteads and pastures were intermingled with the wild crags, forests, and waterfalls.

Baal's River (the name subsequently given by the colonists) is a creek or firth which runs into the land from sixty to seventy miles in a northwesterly direction. A cluster of islands, some hundreds in number, lies in its estuary, and on one of these, named Kangek, the emigrants erected their first dwelling, a house of stones and earth, lined with boards. On the 3rd of August it was completed, and after a short thanksgiving service, in which Egede exhorted his companions from the words of the 117th Psalm, they joyfully removed into it from their narrow quarters on board the ship. Although it was so early in the season, the nights were already very cold. The settlers erected also a blacksmith's forge, and other necessary buildings for their stores and workshops, and named the place Godhaab; *i. e.*, Good hope. An Esquimaux encampment was seen on the neighbouring shore. The people were from four to five feet high, and had broad flat faces, coarse black hair, and a very swarthy complexion. They were clad in seal-skin garments from head to foot, and their tents were also of seal-skin. The proceedings of the Europeans were watched by them with much curiosity; and by their gestures they expressed great surprise at seeing women and children amongst them. They were still more astonished when they perceived that the strangers were building a house, as if they intended to remain in the country: they made signs to them that their house would be buried under the snow; they pointed to the sun, and to the horizon, shivered, closed their eyes, and laid their hands under their heads, intimating by all this that when the winter came they would be all frozen to death, and therefore had better take their departure in good time, before the season of cold and darkness arrived. But when they found that their warnings produced no effect, they became afraid, retired to a more distant part of the coast,

and would not suffer the Europeans to come into
their tents. Gifts and kind treatment allayed
their fears after a time; but several months elapsed
ere they would admit the strangers into their
houses, or would venture to return their visits.
It must be confessed that, excepting for the sake
of doing them good, few Europeans would have
desired to enter a Greenland house, or to admit
the natives into their own. In the concise but
expressive language of one of their early acquaintances, "their clothes dripped with grease and
swarmed with vermin;" and their hands, faces,
furniture, and cooking utensils were alike smeared
with oil, dirt, and seals' fat. The houses in which
they spent the greatest part of the year (the tents
being only used for summer habitations) were long
narrow huts of stone and turf, just high enough
for a man to stand upright. Curtains of seal-skin
served instead of walls to divide the dwelling into
several small compartments, each of which sheltered a separate family. There was no fire, but a
lamp, supplied with filaments of moss for a wick,
and fed with train oil, diffused heat and light
around each compartment. Over each lamp hung
the stone kettle in which the family meals, consisting chiefly of fish, blubber, and seals' flesh,
were cooked. The seal was indeed the one invaluable possession of these poor people, supplying
them with food and clothing, dwellings and boats.
And it was the daily employment of the women to
tan and dress the skins, and to manufacture them

into garments and articles of use and furniture.
The intestines also they made useful, forming with
them a close network which supplied the place of
glass in the windows of their huts, admitting
some degree of light, while it effectually excluded
wind and weather.

Egede took every opportunity of visiting the
natives; and as soon as he found out that "*kina*"
meant What is this? he said *kina? kina?* of every
object he saw, and committed the answers to
paper. In this way he learnt the names of many
things, but in other respects his progress was very
slow at first. The pronunciation of the language
was particularly difficult to Europeans, on account
of the guttural *r*, which was sounded very deep
in the throat, and often pronounced like *k*. A
more serious difficulty arose from the nature of the
language itself. The Greenland tongue was most
copious in words expressive of common objects and
occupations, distinguishing the slightest shades of
difference by appropriate terms, but it had no
words for abstract ideas of any kind. Words were
provided with numerous affixes and suffixes (the
whole number of inflections in each verb, for instance, amounting to one hundred and eighty),
and many words were connected together, so that
the natives could express themselves with strength
and brevity; but this peculiarity occasioned great
trouble to the strangers who wished to learn their
language so as to speak it with ease and fluency.
Perceiving that a native named *Arok* had attached

himself to one of the settlers called *Aaron*, on account of the similarity of their names, Mr. Egede left Aaron, with his own consent, amongst the Esquimaux for a few months; hoping that he might gain some knowledge of the language, and might ascertain from his hosts something of the circumstances of the country, and especially whether they knew of other inhabitants of a race different from their own: for his heart yearned after the long-lost countrymen whom he had come so far to seek. Aaron, however, learnt very little from his native acquaintances, whose continued attempts at thieving irritated him so greatly, that he endeavoured at last to reform them by blows. They in return fell upon him and beat him severely, taking away his gun, lest he should do them mischief with it. But afterwards, becoming afraid, they tried to soothe and coax him, entreating, above all things, that he would not tell his Angekok, lest they should be punished. *Angekok*, in the Greenland tongue, signified *Wise Man*. It was the name given by the natives to certain persons amongst them who assumed the office of diviner, or sorcerer, and of whom they stood in awe. Since the coming of the white men several Angekoks had exhausted their spells upon them, and more particularly upon Mr. Egede, as he appeared to be the person in chief authority; in order, as they said, to bring evil upon the foreigners, and force them to quit the country. But seeing that their sorceries availed nothing, they gave out that Egede himself was a very powerful Angekok.

During the first year the colonists were not very successful, either in their hunting or fishing.

BLACK AUKS ON COAST IN THOUSANDS.

The shores of Baal's River were a great resort of reindeer, and there were many white hares, but both deer and hares were excessively shy. In February, when the frost became very severe, and the sea smoked like an oven, black auks flocked in thousands to the shore; but their flesh was not very acceptable to the Europeans, though better flavoured than that of the other sea-fowl. They had chiefly depended on the fishery for a supplement to the stock of provisions which they brought with them from Norway; but for this year at least they found it less productive than the abundance of the seas in their own country had led them to expect. Seal-catching they were unused to, and they were moreover prejudiced against the use of seals' flesh as food. The extreme cold, which rendered it difficult to stir out of doors without having the hands and face frozen, the want of sufficient exercise, and the long-continued use of dry and salt provisions, induced a general listlessness and depression amongst the colonists, and several were attacked by scurvy. The factor found, much to his morti-fication, that the natives declined to barter their superfluous oil, skins, &c., for the goods he had brought from Bergen; but that in the spring, when a Dutch ship passed Godhaab, and ran into the harbour, the people on board bought more in half an hour than he had been able to obtain from the Greenlanders during the whole winter. The reason of this was, that the Dutch, by many years' commerce with Greenland, had won the confidence of the natives, and knowing exactly what kinds of commodities were most acceptable to the Esquimaux, they stocked their ships accordingly.

May had now returned; the earth was beginning to thaw, and though the snow still fell in frequent showers, the welcome light of the sun was only withdrawn for three hours out of the twenty-four. A profusion of mosses, grass, and various small herbs and flowers showed themselves, and the invaluable scurvy-grass, which had sprung up beneath the snow, restored the health of the invalids. But the non-arrival of the ship which had been expected in the course of this month, with fresh stores of provisions and necessaries from Norway, occasioned extreme discontent. Most of the settlers broke into murmurs against the minister for leading them to that dreary wilderness, and all declared their determination to return to Norway by the ship 'Hope,' which had wintered at Godhaab. Egede was thrown into great perplexity and trouble. He could not remain alone in the country, with a wife and little children, to see them perish before his eyes; yet he could not bear to think of abandoning the work he had as yet scarcely begun, and of giving up that opportunity of publishing the Gospel in Greenland, which he had obtained by the unremitting exertions of many years. All he could obtain of the settlers, however, was to wait until June for the arrival of the store-ship. June came, and three weeks of it passed away, and still no ship arrived. The people now began

to collect all their goods, tools, &c., and to de-
molish their habitations.   With a very sorrowful
heart Egede watched these preparations for de-
serting the country, for he felt almost constrained
to go away too. But his wife withstood this
resolution with so much firmness that, as his
narrative tells us, he even felt ashamed to be so
far her inferior in faith and courage. From the
time of their arrival in Greenland, she had
looked upon it as the place which God had
appointed for her husband and herself, and with
cheerful contentment made light of the privations
and discomforts which they all had to endure.
She was so firmly persuaded that the ship would
arrive sooner or later, that she earnestly remon-
strated with the people who were pulling down
their houses, assuring them that they were giving
themselves needless trouble.   They laughed at
the predictions of " the new prophetess;" but their
incredulity was soon put to the blush.   On the
27th June the long-expected vessel entered the
harbour, bringing abundance of provisions, and
conveying to Mr. Egede the welcome assurance
that the king intended to support the mission to
the utmost of his power.

Encouraged by these joyful tidings, Egede addressed himself with fresh hope to the instruction
of the natives. His little boys were already able
to make themselves understood; and although the
pronunciation, which they acquired almost in-
sensibly, was still extremely difficult to their

father, he had laid up a large stock of Greenlandic
words, and thought that with the help of his children he might begin to discourse more freely
upon religious subjects. Paul, the eldest of
the boys, could draw a little, and his father
directed him to sketch as well as he could some
of the chief occurrences recorded in Scripture.
Paul himself, describing in after-life these first
pictorial attempts at missionary work, assures us
that they were of the very rudest description;
but rough and imperfect as they might be, they
answered in some degree their purpose, which
was that of illustrating Mr. Egede's meaning
when he attempted to relate to the natives the
History of the Creation, the Fall, the Deluge, the
miracles of the Lord Jesus, His death, and resurrection. The Greenlanders were pleased with
anything in the shape of a story; but the miracles
by which Christ healed the sick and raised the
dead found the quickest entrance into their
minds; and as Mr. Egede came to them in the
character of a messenger from this mighty and
beneficent Lord, they imagined that he too
could do many wonderful works. Sick persons
were frequently brought to him, with the request
that he would blow upon them, for that was the
way in which the Angekoks pretended to cure
diseases. Egede was very careful to tell them
that he was but a man like themselves: he could
sometimes direct them (he said) to medicines
useful for their sickness; but God only, his

EGEDE TEACHING IN ESQUIMAUX HUT.

Maker and theirs, could cure them. They must look to Him for health and every good thing which they desired. After speaking thus, he would kneel down and pray for the sick. Several persons by whom he thus prayed, recovered, and the confidence of the natives in the good intentions of the missionary was greatly strengthened, so that they gladly received him into their houses. But when he tried to teach them that there were diseases of the soul as well as of the body, and that all men needed to be healed of *that* sickness, they had no ears to listen : or, if he prevailed on them to give heed to his words for a little while, they would presently answer, that it was very likely Europeans might have sick souls, but that Greenlanders had no such sickness. Let the great God of whom he spoke give them healthy bodies, and send them plenty of seals, and they wanted nothing more.

In order to gain more frequent opportunities of instructing them, and a more accurate knowledge of their character and customs, as well as of their language, Egede took his two boys with him, and lived amongst the natives during a portion of the second winter which he spent in Greenland. It required no little self-denial on the part of the father and his children to bear with patience the many annoyances of such a situation. The strong rancid smell of the train-oil burning in the lamps, and that of the fish and blubber boiling in the kettles, the odour of half-putrid seals' flesh (esteemed a most delicate viand), the sickening effluvia of the skins which the women were tanning, constantly pervaded the huts, and rendered the atmosphere almost unbearable. The general dirtiness of everything and everybody has been already alluded to; the food was no exception. It was cooked and served up without the slightest regard to cleanliness, and torn in pieces with the teeth and fingers. If the natives wished to show particular honour to their visitor, they presented him with a piece of meat or blubber from which they had carefully licked the dirt, and the refusal of this inviting gift was regarded by them as a great affront. Notwithstanding all these unpleasant circumstances, however, Mr. Egede laboured patiently and indefatigably amongst them; and his children, who had caught something of the spirit which animated their parents, endured good - humouredly the many things which they did not like. They soon made companions and playmates of some of the Greenland children, and by constant intercourse with them became quite familiar with their language. They were able now to help their father to translate some portions of the Gospels. The Greenlanders were at first much afraid when he read to them, thinking that he used some kind of witchcraft, and heard a voice proceeding from the book though they did not; and it was long before they would venture to touch a book or a piece of paper with writing on it. But when they saw that no harm happened to them from contact with these formidable things, their fears were succeeded by great admiration, and they esteemed it an honour to carry a letter for any of the settlers; "carrying a voice," they called it.

The missionary observed no trace of religious worship amongst them, excepting that the hunters sometimes, on returning from the chase, laid a piece of the first reindeer which they had killed on a block of stone, to insure (they said) success on a future occasion. They calculated the seasons with tolerable accuracy, by observing the times at which the eider-fowl brooded, and the seals, fishes, and birds returned to their customary haunts. In the summer they divided the days according to the shadow cast by the sun on the rocks and mountains; and in the winter they distinguished the time by the rising and setting of certain stars. Some of their notions about the heavenly bodies were rather poetical, and they gave names of their own to the more conspicuous constellations. Thus the Great Bear was called " *Tukto* "—the reindeer; the Pleiades were dogs hunting a bear the whole night through; Orion was *Sirktuk*—the Bewildered Ones; that constellation consisting of certain seal-hunters, who lost themselves on their way home, and were changed into stars. They computed with sufficient exactness the time of the winter solstice, and celebrated it by a great feast in honour of the sun, to attend at which the natives assembled together from distant places, as to a fair, bringing

with them eider-down, skins, horns of the nar-
whal, and especially vessels of weichstein, a soft
smooth stone of which the Greenlanders made
their lamps and kettles. The days were devoted
to traffic; the nights, which the brilliancy of the
stars and the light of the moon, reflected by the
ice and snow, rendered bright as day, were spent
in feasting and dancing, reciting the exploits of
their ancestors in the seal-hunt, and singing songs
of joy because the sun was about to return. But
there was no act of worship. After Egede had
become much more intimately acquainted with
the people, he learnt that their forefathers had
rendered honour to a Being who lived above the
clouds, and that they themselves believed in
the existence of a Spirit pervading all things
in Heaven and earth, whom they called *Silla*.
They believed also in a great multitude of lesser
spirits, good and evil; but especially in one who
was both good and powerful, and whom they
called Torngarsuk. But they thought it not worth
while to pay him any religious worship, alleging
that he was too benevolent a being to require to
be entreated to do them good. Of their own
natural condition, as sinful, and exposed to the
anger of a Holy, Almighty Creator, they had not
the smallest apprehension.

Although there was much that was disagreeable
and even disgusting in their household economy,
Egede could not help admiring the quietness with
which in general they carried on their daily

occupations; each family in the narrow compartment allotted to them, without intruding on their
neighbours, or quarrelling among themselves.
They were rarely idle; to the women, indeed,
idleness would have been scarcely possible, for
they were at once the butchers, cooks, sempstresses,
tanners, tailors, shoemakers, and builders of the
community; the men concerning themselves only
with hunting and fishing, and the manufacture of
the necessary implements, in which they displayed
great ingenuity. The missionary hoped at first that
their usually quiet and inoffensive deportment arose
from natural kindness and gentleness of heart;
but when he had resided longer in the country,
he was compelled to take a far less favourable
view of their character. Its most pleasing feature
was the strong affection which the parents entertained for their children. While young, they
would scarcely suffer them to go out of their sight;
and instances were known in which, the child
having been drowned, the mother had destroyed
herself, unable to endure the anguish of her be-
reavement. But the strength of their parental,
and in many cases, of their filial affection, was
strangely contrasted with their hard, careless
indifference to the sorrows and sufferings of persons less nearly connected with them. Egede had
admired their readiness to entertain strangers, but
he discovered that this apparent hospitality rarely
proceeded from other than selfish motives; they
literally gave to "receive as much again," and to

the needy were extremely ungenerous. Orphans, and widows whose children were too young to be serviceable in seal-catching, rarely met with assistance and compassion. On the contrary, they were commonly plundered of their most valuable goods as soon as their natural protector was dead, and after protracting a miserable existence as long as they could by means of fishes, mussels, and sea-weed, fell victims to cold and starvation. Often, when a kayak was overset at sea, the people on shore would stand and look on with the utmost unconcern if its occupant was not a friend of their own; they could even amuse themselves with watching his struggles as he vainly buffeted with the waves, and would rather see him sink and perish before their eyes than take the trouble of putting off in another kayak to save him. In these and other respects a wonderful and beautiful change of character was observable when the light and love of the Gospel was shed abroad in the hearts of the Greenlanders. But there was yet a long time to wait for that day of blessing, and Egede, labouring still in patient hope, looked in vain for the first streaks of the dawning.

At times they resented the endeavours of the missionary to teach them, and would interrupt him by their noisy merriment, or turn what he said into ridicule. Some of the colonists, incensed at these impertinences, threatened to chastise them severely; but Egede preferred the milder method of forbearance and friendly expostulation, and effected so much that the Greenlanders entirely desisted from their unseemly interruptions, though hearing they heard, and did not understand. He had invited two orphan lads to come and live with him, and by dint of many presents and much kindness prevailed on them to begin to learn to read and write. Seeing, however, that a quiet life, such as Europeans led, was very irksome to them, he did not forbid their going to sea, or visiting their native acquaintances when they desired to do so ; but notwithstanding this freedom, they soon became tired even of the slight degree of restraint which their new occupations imposed upon them, and objected that there was nothing to be gained by looking on a book or making marks upon paper with a feather, whereas they could get both food and amusement by catching seals and shooting birds. Mr. Egede took great pains to set forth the advantages of being able to read and write, that men could thus know the thoughts of an absent friend, and as it were speak to him; and, above all, that by this means they might learn the goodness of God and His will from the Bible. But these were benefits which they had no desire to enjoy, and as soon as they had obtained everything that they wished for, they stole away without telling the missionary that they were going. Several persons asked him to take them in for a time, and though this was very inconvenient to himself and his wife, who had little more room than they needed for the accommodation of their own family, they would not refuse, for they hoped that their unbidden guests might gain some good from living in a Christian household. Sometimes as many as eight or ten Greenlanders would take up their abode at Godhaab; but their motive for coming was only that they might be comfortably provided for while the season was not favourable for hunting and fishing. They listened, indeed, while Egede endeavoured to teach them out of the Scriptures, and some of them could even answer correctly several questions relating to Christian doctrine; but not one appeared to have the least real understanding or feeling of the truths which their lips uttered. And when they had received food and shelter as long as they desired, they took their leave.

The winter proved to be the time in which Mr. Egede had most opportunity of pursuing his missionary labours. From time to time the company of merchants at Bergen, and also the king, sent directions that the country should be explored, in order to find out the dwelling-places of the old Norwegians, and to plant new settlements in the spots which seemed most favourable for hunting and fishing; and the labour of planning and conducting these voyages of discovery fell principally to the lot of Egede, as superintendent of the colony. Often, therefore, during the short summer he was obliged to leave his family at Godhaab, while he accompanied exploring parties to various parts of the coast. His first object was to find out a more suitable spot for the Godhaab settlement on the mainland, and where the ground admitted of cultivation. South of Baal's River he passed under a lofty three-peaked mountain, visible from one hundred miles at sea, and entitled ("*Hiorte Tuk*") The Stag's Horn; and beyond this came to a fine creek, where there was great abundance of herbage and brushwood, a salmon Elv or brook, and excellent pasturage. The colonists named this place Priester Fiord (the Priest's Firth), and were well pleased to remove to so verdant a valley. But after they had dug stones, and made preparations for building, they were obliged to desist, for the creek proved too difficult of entrance to be safe for ships. Close by the mouth of this fiord there was another, on the shores of which both seals and reindeer were seen in abundance; and here Egede discovered the first traces of his lost countrymen, the ruins of ancient Norwegian villages. The remains of the churches were easily distinguished; they had evidently been very solidly built of the freestone which was plentiful in that neighbourhood. In other places similar remains were found from time to time. Ascending Baal's River, to view a spot where the Greenlanders informed him seals might be killed by hundreds, Egede came to a very pretty valley, in which stood the lower portion of a square tower, and a large long heap of ruins near it, which appeared to be the remains of the church

E

where, four hundred years before, the inhabitants of the valley had assembled to worship God. Many lesser buildings were met with; and the ground was thickly clothed with grass, and overgrown with dwarf elder-trees, birch, willow, and juniper. The bright blossoms of the creeping crimson azalea, and many small but beautiful wild flowers, enlivened the scene, and looking seawards, it appeared as pleasant a spot as man might hope to find in those far northern regions. But the prospect on the land side presented a dismal contrast; it was a waste of ice stretching as far as eye could reach. In succeeding years, Egede and other Europeans, going farther towards the south, discovered many such places, and found traces of cultivation. Fragments of earthen vessels, bones, and many pieces of the bells which had once called the people to public worship, were picked up amongst the ruins and herbage. But of the people themselves, none remained. Those children of his countrymen whom Egede had been so desirous to succour had long since passed away from the face of the earth. *How* they perished could never be known; but the tradition of the natives respecting their disappearance was probably not far from the truth; though the hereditary hatred of the Esquimaux for the enemies of their ancestors had invested the story with supernatural features, as that the *Kablunaet* (or foreigners) were dogs transformed into the likeness of men. The forefathers of the Esquimaux, whom they proudly termed *Innuit*, that is, *Men*, were brave hunters; but they were treated with contempt by the Kablunaet, and in revenge they waged war against them, and after a long while destroyed them all. In Denmark it was long supposed that more important remains of the ancient settlements existed on the east coast, and Mr. Egede was early directed to send some resolute sailors to explore that part of the country. Being much concerned to see this commission faithfully executed, he set out himself with two shallops, and reached Staatenhuk. But the voyage proved difficult and dangerous; and the seamen were so alarmed by the tempestuous weather that the missionary could not prevail on them to advance any farther. Soon after returning from this expedition he accompanied a party northwards, to seek a good situation for the whale fishery. He was able, though not at the first attempt, to accomplish this object; but the season was unusually rigorous, and the missionary and his companions did not reach home again until after several weeks of excessive fatigue and exposure to the piercing cold, the ice having blocked up the sounds, and extending also in immense fields over the open sea. Many stations of Greenlanders were visited in the course of these expeditions. At first they were afraid of the foreigners; but when the native pilot who accompanied them told his countrymen that the great Angekok of the Kablunaet was with them, they received the explorers with singing and shouts of joy, and followed them from place to place, hoping to see some wonderful thing done. They even conducted the missionary to a grave, begging him to raise the corpse which it contained. At another place a blind man was led in by his friends, to have his sight restored. Egede, however, perceived that this was not a case which required the exercise of miraculous power, and having exhorted the man to trust in God only to make the means he was going to use effectual for his cure, he applied to the eyes something which he thought would do them good. Several years afterwards the man came to Godhaab to thank the missionary for having restored his sight.

In the summer of 1723, Mr. Egede was joined by another missionary, Albert Top, who ministered to the colonists at Godhaab in his absence, and also applied himself very diligently to learn the native tongue. Egede had already prepared as well as he could some helps for his fellow-labourers and successors, and he improved them from time to time as his knowledge of the language increased. He drew up a translation of the Creed, the Ten Commandments, and some short prayers in Greenlandic; he also prepared some short easy lessons in Scripture truth, illustrating them by similes and parables, a mode of instruction which he perceived to be particularly acceptable to the natives. They were greatly pleased to hear of the soul's immortality, and of the resurrection. They had received from their Angekoks various descriptions of the future state of the soul; some affirming that it successively inhabited several bodies on earth; and others, that it went to a happy hunting-ground, covered with everlasting verdure, and peopled with animals innumerable; but this pleasant world, they asserted, could only be reached by a rough and painful journey. They listened eagerly while Egede spoke of the resurrection, when soul and body should again become one, never more to be separated; and were delighted to hear of that fair land where there would be no more cold, or darkness, no hunger, sickness, sorrow, or death. But of the crowning happiness of Heaven, that there is no sin there—they had no appreciation whatever. When they had become tolerably familiar with the subjects on which the missionary discoursed to them, they would say, " We believe all that—tell us something new." They were surprised and angry when he assured them that indeed they believed it not, or they would be quite differently affected by it: they would stand in awe of the Holy, Almighty, and Most Merciful God who had made them; they would see that they were sinful men before Him; would be sorry and ashamed, and would long to have their sins forgiven, and their hearts so changed that they might please Him, and obey all His commandments. One day when Egede was speaking of the command which the Lord Jesus gave to His disciples, that they should go and teach all nations, baptizing them in the name of the

Father, and of the Son, and of the Holy Ghost,
the whole company flocked about him, desiring to
be baptized ; and were astonished that he refused.
He had but too many proofs that their readiness
to hear the doctrine which he preached, and to
profess their belief in it, was only prompted by
motives of covetousness : they desired to recommend themselves to the missionary and his countrymen, that they might share more largely in the
gifts and advantages which the Europeans had to
bestow. The Angekoks, who saw plainly that, if
the doctrine preached by Mr. Egede were generally
believed, their craft would come to an end, were
foremost in stirring up opposition and ridicule.
Yet when great trouble overtook them they could
not help betraying their belief in the God of the
missionary. An Angekok whose child was very
sick, brought it to Egede, that he might ask his
God to cure it. The missionary saw that the
infant was dying, and told the father so ; but he
added, if you will suffer me to give up your child
to God, He will receive it, and will give it a better
life in Heaven. The man assented, and Egede baptized the little one, who breathed its last shortly
afterwards. When the parents had mourned for
it, after the manner of the Greenlanders, with loud
cries and wailings, they entreated the missionary
to carry it to the grave, for the father thought no
one else was worthy to do so now. He willingly
complied with their request, and interred the poor
babe as a member of the Christian family, with a

feeling of thankfulness that it was placed beyond the reach of harm. When the funeral was over, the Angekok and his wife desired to be baptized too. He explained to them that they, being able to understand the Word of God, must believe it heartily, and be willing to give themselves up to the service of Christ, and then he would joyfully baptize them. But this saying was too hard for them, and they went away.

Amongst the natives whom Egede had received at Godhaab with much kindness, and whom he had instructed in the Gospel as far as he had opportunity, were two youths who became so friendly with the Europeans, that they were willing to go to Denmark by one of the ships which visited Godhaab. He promoted this visit, in the hope that their minds would be opened and quickened by the sight of so much that was new, and that they would on their return convey to their countrymen a clearer notion of European life and civilization than the Greenlanders would ever obtain from the conversation of foreigners. One of these young men died at Bergen, on his way home; but the other, whose name was *Poek*, returned after a year's residence in Denmark, to astonish his countrymen with his account of the royal state of the king, and the splendour of his court, of the great buildings of the city of Copenhagen, the fine ships, and the multitude of soldiers he had seen. He had been very kindly entertained, and had brought back with him many valuable presents, which pleased his countrymen. But the description of the king's military power struck them most forcibly; for hitherto they had esteemed the man who could catch the most seals as the greatest and mightiest lord on earth; and when they heard from Poek that the monarch who possessed all this wealth, and had so many thousand fighting men at his command, listened respectfully to his pastors, though they were his own subjects, when they declared to him the will of the Almighty, the natives began to form some new and awful ideas of the greatness of God.

Pleased, however, as Poek had been with Denmark, he quickly relapsed into the Greenland way of living, and even meditated a migration towards the south, where he would have been quite out of the way of instruction. After many expostulations he was prevailed on to remain and settle at Godhaab; but his European friends as well as himself were obliged to plead for his acceptance with the young woman whom he proposed to marry, so averse was this Greenland damsel to take for her husband a man who had degraded himself by his outlandish way of living. It may be observed, in passing, that the Greenlanders had a remarkably high opinion of themselves; when they wanted to express high approbation of a foreigner, they would say, " He is almost as well behaved as we are ;" or, " He begins to be a man," meaning *a Greenlander*.

After Poek and his companions had departed to

Denmark, Mr. Egede took two younger lads into
his family. They were of promising disposition
and good capacity, and he hoped by God's blessing
to train them up to be teachers of their countrymen. One of them died while still very young;
the other grew up a thoughtful, docile youth, and
became a useful helper in the work of the mission.
After a year's residence at Godhaab, he accompanied Mr. Egede's colleague to the spot selected
for a whaling station on the island of Nepisene;
where, after careful instruction, he was baptized
by the name of Frederic Christian.

The charge imposed on Egede, of rendering the
colony profitable in a mercantile point of view,
greatly added to his labours and anxieties. The
colonists were still but very moderately successful
in their trading, hunting, and fishing pursuits.
Egede tried the experiment of cultivating the
ground in several places. He thawed the earth
to a sufficient depth by setting the long grass
which covered it on fire, and then sowed the grain,
which grew very well till it was in ear, but was
invariably destroyed by night frosts before it had
time to ripen. He also caused search to be made
for ores and minerals; but although Greenland is
by no means wanting in these, nothing could be
obtained which was commercially valuable. The
settlement at Nepisene proved another source of
disappointment. As soon as the winter was over,
Mr. Egede made a voyage thither, and found all
the people in good health. though they had as yet

done little or nothing in fishing, owing, they said, to the extreme severity of the weather. But the men who had emigrated to Greenland were not, for the most part, well suited for the career they had chosen; and when they found that they must labour as hard as at home, and endure more hardship if they wished to prosper, they became discontented.

The summer had no sooner set in than the colonists at Nepisene, instead of exerting themselves to turn the season to account by diligent attention to the fishery, determined with one consent to abandon the settlement. A ship bringing stores and provisions from Norway arrived just at this time; but the people were so bent upon relinquishing their undertaking, that this seasonable supply of their wants had no effect upon them; and to the extreme grief and vexation of Mr. Egede, they returned in this very ship to Godhaab, pleading as an excuse that the provisions were not in sufficient quantity to last for twelve months.

The trouble and expense laid out in the preceding year upon the buildings at Nepisene, which had been constructed with materials brought from Norway, were thus entirely thrown away; and soon afterwards news arrived at Godhaab that the Dutch, or other foreign traders, had wantonly destroyed the whole. Egede could not but fear that the company of merchants would soon grow weary of an undertaking which had hitherto proved so unprofitable; for not only had much money been wasted upon the Nepisene settlement, but several vessels despatched by the company to Godhaab had been wrecked or driven back by storms.

For the present, however, the minds of the missionaries and their companions were occupied by apprehensions of an evil nearer at hand. During a trading voyage to the south, the factor, Jentoft, encountered an Angekok who was practising his magical arts against him and his people. Irritated by the man's impostures and insolent demeanour, he was so indiscreet as to strike him. The enraged Angekok instantly seized his bow and arrows, but was restrained by his countrymen from attempting any violence at that time. By the factor the circumstance was quickly forgotten ; but the Angekok, longing for revenge, formed a plan for cutting off all the Europeans in the country. He had obtained by his reputed success as a magician, great influence over his countrymen in the south ; and by promising them the plunder of the strangers, and representing that it would be easy to destroy them when divided into small parties, he easily induced a considerable number of the natives to engage in the plot. It was known that the factor, with part of the people, would soon be proceeding to the north ; his assistant, with another party, would be engaged in a trading voyage southwards ; and but a few men would be left with the missionary at Godhaab. The conspiracy might probably have succeeded, had it not come to the knowledge of a Greenland boy, whom Egede had taken into his service

some time before. Not liking the restraints imposed on him in a civilized household, he had run
away, and migrated with some of his people to
a distant part of the coast. Here he heard the
plot talked over, and was sufficiently shocked and
alarmed by it to steal away from his companions,
and return secretly to Godhaab, where he revealed
all to the missionary. Egede immediately set a
watch to patrol the settlement day and night,
and took all other precautions which were in his
power, until the return of the factor from the
north relieved him of a portion of his anxieties.
He was still, however, not a little disquieted by the
protracted absence of the factor's assistant; but he
too returned in safety, having been unusually de-
layed, and warned repeatedly by friendly natives
not to have any dealings with their countrymen
at certain places on the south. The Angekok,
finding the Europeans on their guard, had been
obliged to forego his proposed revenge for the
present at least; and he being afterwards captured
by the factor, his adherents were effectually intimi-
dated. He was not, however, punished otherwise
than by imprisonment: and on making submission,
with promise of good behaviour for the time to
come, he was set at liberty. No sooner were their
fears on this account dissipated, than the settlers
found cause for apprehensions of another kind.

The accustomed yearly supply of provisions had
not yet arrived from Norway, though the season
was far advanced. The watchers, looking out

anxiously day by day for the store-ship, were alarmed at observing the wreck of a vessel, surrounded by quantities of ice, driving near the shore. Fearing that this might be the ship which had been loaded with provisions, and that possibly no other might reach them that year, Mr. Egede went one hundred leagues northwards, to the rendezvous of the Dutch whalers, hoping to purchase food from them. The Dutchmen, however, were bound for the American coast, and expecting to be several weeks at sea, were afraid to part with more than a very small portion of their stock of food. For a short time the colonists were almost in a state of famine; eight persons being obliged to put up with the allowance of one. They tried to obtain seals from the Greenlanders, to boil with their oatmeal; but the natives, with their usual selfishness, took advantage of their needy condition, and refused to sell them any. Happily the scarcity did not continue long. Late in the year a vessel arrived, having on board ample supplies; but the captain informed them that a ship previously despatched had been wrecked; and his own progress had been so much impeded by the ice, that he would not venture back to Norway until the following spring. By this time the merchants at Bergen were, as Egede had foreseen, tired of an undertaking which had involved them in so many losses and disappointments. The ships which arrived in the summer of 1727 brought word that the company had disengaged themselves from the

Greenland trade; but they also brought the encouraging assurance that the king **was** resolved to support the mission notwithstanding the present unpromising aspect of affairs. He had therefore sent out a commissary, charged to confer with the factor upon the best methods of promoting the mercantile progress of the colony. By this arrangement, Mr. Egede gladly found himself relieved from the harassing secular business which had demanded so large a portion of his time ; but he was deprived at this period, of the assistance of his colleague, Mr. Top, who had laboured with exemplary diligence during his four years' residence in the country. His health had now become so enfeebled that he was forced to seek a less rigorous climate.

Deprived of other help, Egede availed himself more largely of the services of his son Paul, who was now about eighteen years of age, and was looking forward to be himself a missionary at some future day. His father saw with pleasure that he had entirely won the goodwill of the natives, and from his early familiarity with their language, was able to render his conversation and instructions acceptable to them. But the missionary had still the grief to see, that although a certain knowledge of Scripture truth had been imparted more or less to many persons, and by their constant journeyings and migrations had become pretty widely diffused along the coast, it was a merely historical knowledge, which did not affect the conduct or the feelings. Of all the adults to

whom he had declared the Gospel during the
space of seven years, but one man had appeared
really to believe it ; this was Poek, whose visit to
Copenhagen has been mentioned on a former page.
In 1728, Egede baptized him and his wife. He
had observed more hopeful results among the
young, many of whom had been attracted by his
kindness to listen regularly to his teaching ; and
some he thought had received the truth into their
hearts. At present it was still but the seed-time ;
hardly could he perceive, here and there, one
tender blade beginning to sprout upwards ; but he
remembered that it had been often thus : for "one
man soweth, and another reapeth."

King Frederic had embraced the cause of Greenland with remarkable zeal. He was making dis-
positions not only to uphold the mission as at present, but to plant missionaries at various points
of the coast, and colonies for the cultivation of
the land. Four vessels were despatched from Copenhagen in the year 1728. They brought two
missionaries and a large party of colonists, consisting of masons, carpenters, and mechanics of all
descriptions; herdsmen also, with flocks of sheep
and cattle to be pastured in the sheltered valleys
during the brief summer, and housed and tended
within doors through all the nine months' winter.
There were also building materials for erecting a
settlement and a port ; with cannon and am-
munition, and a sufficient garrison under the
charge of two superior officers, one of whom was

to be governor, and the other commandant. It
appeared, however, that the nature of the country
was still very imperfectly understood at Copenhagen, for the officers were provided with horses,
with which to travel over the mountains, recon-
noitre the inland country, and if possible discover
the principal settlements of the ancient colonists,
which then, and for one hundred years afterwards,
were confidently believed to have been on the coast
facing Iceland.

The first care of the governor was to remove the
settlement of Godhaab to the mainland, about ten
miles farther to the east, and to enlarge it with the
necessary buildings. But the ill success which
had hitherto attended the efforts made for the
advancement of the colony, followed the well-
conceived plan of the king, and defeated his
benevolent intentions. The authorities at Copenhagen had made an unwise selection of emigrants.
Some, indeed (and the most useful), were artisans
and labourers who had volunteered for the enterprise ; but others were convicts, who had been
taken out of the house of correction, provided
with wives, and sent over to cultivate the country.
To both classes of emigrants the confinement and
inaction of their life on ship-board had been
sufficiently trying; and the wet, unwholesome
weather which they encountered on landing served
still farther to nourish a spirit of depression and
discontent. The season was unusually cold
and rainy; its evil effect upon their health was

aggravated by the irregular living in which they
found opportunity to indulge, while the arrangements of the intended colony were still unsettled
and the regulations for its government not put into
force. The consequence was a contagious disorder,
which quickly extended itself, and carried off, not
only the unruly and intemperate members of the
community, but the most useful mechanics and
workmen. In the general sickness and mortality
which prevailed, the cattle failed to receive the
care which was indispensable for their preservation
in such a climate, and they also perished. These
troubles were greatly enhanced by a mutiny among
the soldiers. Disgusted with a country which
afforded them so much less scope for indulgence
than they had been used to at home, they broke into
a rebellion which threatened not only the lives of
their officers, but those of the missionaries, for they
regarded them as the authors of their banishment.
The malady which was raging ended the mutiny
by cutting off the ringleaders ; but it was not until
the spring of 1729 that the health and peace of the
settlement were restored ; and by that time, the
greater number of the emigrants had found a grave
beneath the snow. The death of many useful and
well-disposed labourers was a heavy blow : with
respect to the mutinous and disorderly characters
who had perished, it was felt that their prolonged
life would probably have been a greater evil to the
colony than the contagious sickness which had
carried them off. Certain of the women, especially,

F

who had accepted the offer of emigration to escape from prison, had misconducted themselves so grossly as to call forth the contemptuous scoffs of the natives, who, whatever their real character might be, were seldom guilty of unbecoming conduct in public.

As soon as the sickness was at an end, and order had been restored, the governor, Major Paars, with a few of the men who remained to him, made an attempt to cross the mountains, and penetrate to the east side, as the king had enjoined him. The horses were all dead, but that was of the less consequence, since the explorers quickly discovered that it would have been impossible to travel over such ground on horseback. The whole country was overspread with ice so slippery and uneven that they could not even stand upon it, and rifted in clefts of various width, out of which the water gushed in torrents with a loud roar. A recent English navigator, Sir Leopold M'Clintock, has found reason to believe that by observing the variations in the surface of the glacier, avoiding the clefts, and following the windings between them, the interior of Greenland might be reached. But at the point where Major Paars and his company attempted to cross, this seems to have been impracticable; and after an absence of nearly a fortnight, they returned, hopeless of success, to Godhaab. Foiled in the endeavour to discover a suitable spot on the east side of the country, the governor and commandant now took measures for

KAPPAROKTOLIK GLACIER.

re-erecting the abandoned settlement on the island of Nepisene, and strengthening it with a fort. And they were gratified by an encouraging message from the king, who sent them also ships laden with timber, and other necessaries.

Missionary operations had been greatly impeded during the last year. The Greenlanders had been alarmed by the influx of Europeans; and the arrival of the soldiers in particular had aroused their fears and suspicions. It was a great relief to them when they saw so many of the newly-arrived emigrants carried off by the sickness; and they attributed this happy result to the incantations of a famous Angekok who had persuaded them that he could destroy the Kablunaet. But seeing that some of the fighting-men whom they so much dreaded remained alive, the greater number of them migrated to Disko Bay, far to the north of Godhaab; and thus, to the great grief of Egede, placed themselves for the present quite beyond the reach of Christian instruction. There were, however, many natives living on the islands in Baal's River, and not a few of these professed their belief in the word which the missionary preached to them, though he could see no evidence that it was a belief unto righteousness. He thought that if these people would suffer him to baptize their young children, on the understanding that they would not remove them afterwards from the neighbourhood of the mission, he, and the colleagues who had lately joined him, might be able to train up these little ones in the knowledge and fear of God, and perhaps the children in their turn might help to bring their parents within the fold of Christ's Church. He submitted this plan to the College of Missions at Copenhagen. They agreed to it, on condition that the parents should distinctly understand that Baptism was offered to their children as a means of blessing to the soul, not as a means of health or strength to the body; and that they should freely consent to their Baptism and instruction in the Christian religion, without being in any way allured by presents or prospects of temporal advantage. In the year 1729, Mr. Egede began to put this design into execution by baptizing sixteen little children belonging to families who dwelt in the isles of Kookörnen; the parents being not only ready to offer them, but even requesting to be baptized themselves—a request which the missionary would have been but too happy to grant, had he seen any reason to believe that it proceeded from an enlightened heart. From these islands he proceeded to others, and had soon a little flock in several places, whom he visited and taught. The native children were by no means deficient in quickness. They were very volatile, but if their attention could be secured they made rapid progress; and Egede was rejoiced to find that some of his young disciples readily retained the lessons he taught them, and appeared to comprehend them quite as well as could be expected at their tender age. Mr. Egede's beloved pupil, Frederic Christian, was of great use to him now. Often when he would have visited his little scholars he was detained from them by other calls of duty. At such times he deputed Frederic to give them a lesson, and sometimes also sent him to read the portions of Scripture which he had translated to their parents.

The second summer after the arrival of the governor was distinguished by a scarcity similar to that which had occurred in 1726, and owing to a similar cause—the detention of the store-ship by ice and storms. When it at length arrived, it was found to be laden not only with the necessary provisions, but with all kinds of building materials, for the erection of houses in the valleys formerly peopled by the Norwegians; and it was the design of the king to transplant families from Iceland to inhabit them. Hardly, however, had the vessel unloaded her cargo, and the governor been made aware of the king's intention, when the spring which set in motion all these plans for the benefit of Greenland was suddenly stopped by the death of Frederic IV. His successor, Christian VI., seeing that all the schemes of colonization and commerce which had been attempted had disappointed the hopes of their projectors, and that little success had attended the efforts made for the conversion of the natives, issued a mandate that the settlements of Godhaab and Nepisene should be abandoned, and all the colonists should return to their own country. It was left to Mr. Egede's own choice to return with them or to remain in Greenland. In case he remained, he might keep as many of the people as chose to stay with him, and provisions to last for one year; but he was warned to expect no farther assistance from Denmark. This was indeed a grievous discouragement to the long-cherished hopes of the missionary. None of the colonists were willing to remain; and of the sailors who would have been of real use to him, the captains of the ships declared they could not spare one.

He would thus have been left alone to provide for the sustenance of his family, without other assistance than that of his second son, Niels, a youth of eighteen or nineteen. Paul had gone to Copenhagen in 1728, and was still there, pursuing his studies for the ministry. Under these circumstances there seemed little hope that Egede could continue his labours for the good of the natives. Yet he could not bear to relinquish them, and least of all could he make up his mind to desert the little flock of children whom he had baptized and taught. Happily there was not room in the ships to carry away all the goods belonging to the inhabitants of the two settlements, and as it was apparent that everything which was left behind, not excepting the buildings themselves, would become a prey to the Greenlanders or to foreign traders as soon as the ships had departed, Mr. Egede prevailed on the captains to leave ten seamen for their protection. He undertook, with the assistance of his son Niels, to carry on the trade with the natives, that the government might receive some compensation for the expense of sending a ship to Greenland in the following year. His two colleagues and the rest of the people now took their departure, and six Greenlanders accompanied them to Copenhagen.

Soon after they had sailed, and before Egede could provide for the removal or safe custody of the buildings and stores left at Nepisene, a party of Dutch or other foreign traders, finding the place unpeopled, and prompted as before by mercantile jealousy, set fire to it, and consumed the whole. This was bad; but a more serious cause of sorrow and vexation was the conduct of the parents whose children had been baptized. Unmindful of their promise to remain near God-haab, they yielded this year to the love of wandering, which was a marked feature of the native character, and migrated to distant parts of the coast. For some time before this migration took place, Egede had found unusual difficulty in collecting the children for instruction; the parents frequently hiding them, and refusing to let them go to the missionary, on the pretext that they were afraid he meant to carry them away. They were perhaps afraid lest their children should become too well affected to European notions, and refuse to conform to Greenland habits when they grew older.

The series of toils, vexations, and anxieties through which Egede had passed since his arrival in Greenland had greatly impaired his bodily strength. His mental vigour might well have failed also; but he possessed an unfailing source of refreshment in the loving sympathy of his family, and above all in the Christian hope which animated the spirit of his wife. This truly excellent woman had endured much in the course of her Greenland life; had been subjected to many privations, and at times to much actual suffering; but she had never repined, **never** uttered a word which savoured of discouragement, or breathed regret for the loss of former enjoyments. However oppressed her husband might be by the multiplied obstacles which beset his path and defeated his efforts for the spiritual welfare of the natives, his burdens were lightened and rendered tolerable by her lively sympathy and enduring fortitude. "Our God called us away from our country and our father's house to come hither; and He will never fail us," was the thought which soothed all her fears and sorrows. By her tender ingenuity and watchful care her children found their ice-surrounded Greenland home full of happiness; and all who came within her reach, whether Europeans or natives, had a part in her benevolent deeds.

Niels Egede was an invaluable helper to his father at this time; both in conducting the necessary traffic with the Greenlanders, and in taking pains to instruct the natives whom he met with on his trading excursions. And by his exertions, and those of the sailors who had been left in the country, and who were content to act under his command, a larger cargo of oil and blubber was procured this year than in any of the former ones, in which so many more persons had been engaged and so much expense incurred. Niels and his crew would have been more successful still, had they not lost two of their largest boats in a storm, just at the season when the trade was in its fullest activity.

Meanwhile, the new king, Christian VI., though he had not promised any farther aid to the mission, had come to the conclusion that Mr. Egede's persevering and strenuous exertions deserved some support. He sent him, in 1732, the necessary supplies for one more year, and when that was expired, and he was in much suspense as to the future, his heart was rejoiced by the arrival of a ship bringing the welcome intelligence that the king meant to recommence and uphold the Greenland mission. In this ship arrived two young Moravian missionaries from Germany, accompanied by an older brother, who came to assist them in preparing a dwelling, and otherwise providing for themselves. They had obtained the king's permission to labour in Greenland, and brought with them a letter written by his own hand, in which he recommended them to the friendly offices of Mr. Egede. Even without this token of the royal favour, their desire to promote the best interests of the natives would have insured them the regard of the veteran missionary. He received them with cordial goodwill, and gave them all the assistance in his power towards the acquisition of the language, as well as all the little additions to their necessary comforts which he and his wife had it in their power to bestow. These missionaries (Frederick Bœhnioch and Matthew Stach) were destined to take an important part in the evangelizing of Greenland (and an account of their labours, and of the success with which they were rewarded, will be found in another memoir, that of Matthew Stach); but the first year of their residence in the country was marked by a darker and deeper cloud than any which had yet rested upon Greenland. Of the six natives who had been carried to Denmark in 1731, two only survived; and to these, also, the change of climate, or of living, seemed to be so injurious, that they were sent back to their own country by one of the ships despatched from Copenhagen in the summer of 1733. One died on the voyage; the other recovered health and strength, and landed at Godhaab to all appearance perfectly well. He set off almost immediately to visit his friends and kindred, who were scattered in various islands and along the coast; and nothing more was heard of him until two or three weeks afterwards, when he was brought back to Godhaab, dying. Mr. Egede saw at once that he had the small-pox, and sent messengers instantly to all the places round Godhaab to warn the inhabitants not to come within reach of infection, or if they had unhappily already caught it, not to leave their own homes. But no warnings proved of any avail. The poor boy had already unconsciously communicated the disease to several persons; but the natives had never seen the small-pox before, and could not at first believe that they must take any particular precaution against the spread of the disorder. The disease, however, quickly assumed its most virulent form. Scarcely one of the natives in that part of the country escaped the infection, and very few of those who were attacked recovered. The first who died was Frederic Christian, to the great sorrow of Mr. Egede, who had instructed him and watched over him with fatherly kindness for the last nine years. But of this, his son in the Gospel, he could hope that he had but fallen asleep in Christ. No such hope cheered the sad scenes of which he was now the daily witness. It was in vain that he, his son Niels, and the German missionaries continually went about, carrying with them such means of relief as they possessed, and imploring the people to abstain from things which they knew must be hurtful to them. The unhappy creatures would listen to no persuasion. Impatient of the excruciating pain, heat, and thirst which they were enduring, they could not be restrained from continually drinking iced water; and owing, Egede thought, to this, they seldom outlived the third day. Several stabbed themselves, or plunged into the sea, to put a speedier end to their sufferings. While her husband and his companions were visiting the people at their houses, Mrs. Egede turned her house into an hospital, and received all who fled to her, till every room was filled with the sick and dying, whom, with the help of her family, she nursed night and day. Between the months of September and January five hundred persons died in the neighbourhood of Baal's River, and but eight recovered. Wherever the mission-

MRS. EGEDE NURSING SICK AT HER HOUSE.

aries went, they were shocked by the sight of
houses tenanted only by the corpses of their
former occupants, and of dead bodies lying un-
buried on the snow. To these they rendered the
last charity of a grave, by covering them with
stones. The Greenlanders were in general particularly solicitous about the burial of their dead,
but in the present distress these cares were forgotten. One remarkable instance of calm fore-

thought on the part of a dying man came to the notice of Egede. The only living creatures found on one island were a little girl, covered with small-pox, and three younger brothers. The father had buried all the rest of his family and neighbours; and feeling that he had not long to live, had prepared a grave of stones, in which he laid himself down, and bade his little daughter cover him over with skins, first telling her that he had provided a supply of food for her and her brothers, consisting of two dead seals and some dried herrings, upon which they were to live till they could get to the place where the Europeans were. The sickness lasted till the summer of 1734, extending over a considerable portion of the country. More than two thousand persons died, and for many leagues north and south of Godhaab the land was depopulated. The pity and care which the sufferers experienced at the hands of Egede and his family touched the hearts of some amongst them. One who had been bitterly opposed to the missionary and his teaching, said to him in his dying moments, " You have been kinder to us than we have been to one another. You have tended us in our sickness, fed us when we were famishing, buried our dead, who would else have been a prey to dogs and ravens. And you have told us of God, and of a better life to come." In some of the children whom he had baptized and taught, Egede was much comforted to perceive a spirit of patient resignation, and a happy hope of the resurrection to life. But amongst the older natives, too many refused all exhortation and comfort. "We have called on God to help," said some of these, "and no help came;" and they vented their despair in wild cries and revilings.

The pestilence was hardly over, when a ship arrived from Denmark, having on board three missionaries, one of whom was Paul Egede. He was to be stationed at a new settlement about to be founded at Disko Bay. For the present, however, he remained at Godhaab, to comfort and assist his parents, who were almost worn out with the distressing scenes of the last nine months. It appeared very improbable that Mr. Egede would ever recover sufficient strength to resume the laborious duties of his mission; but it was thought that a change of climate might in part at least restore his health and that of his wife. Both of them desired to take their young daughters to Europe, that they might enjoy some advantages of education which could not be afforded them in Greenland. But before any arrangements could be made for their departure, Mrs. Egede was attacked by a painful and lingering disease. After several months of suffering, borne in the same spirit of faith and patience which had governed her life, she entered into rest, December 21st, 1736. This last and heaviest sorrow almost overwhelmed the spirit of her husband. Utterly broken down in health, he fell into such a state of depression as greatly alarmed his children. He says of himself that a great darkness fell upon him. He felt as if he were so far from God that he could not even bear to hear the Scriptures read, or to be present at Divine worship. But he suffered in silence, and none knew how deep his distress was, until one night when his children overheard him lamenting in tones of anguish that his God had forsaken him. They came about him with anxious affection, and brought his fellow-labourers to comfort him with prayers and good words; but his soul refused comfort. After a time these seasons of mental agony became less frequent and acute. He exerted himself as well as he was able for the benefit of the people; and before leaving the colony, recovered sufficient strength to preach to them for the last time, taking for his text these words: "I said, I have laboured in vain; I have spent my strength for nought, and in vain; yet surely my judgment is with the Lord, and my work with my God." (Isaiah xlix. 4.)

He yet had hope that God would make His ways known to this people; and there were some indications, scarcely perceived as yet, that the Word of Truth, which had so long been preached to them, was beginning to excite serious thoughts in a few at least. Not many weeks before, a stranger, coming from a distant spot on the south coast, had visited Mr. Egede, who received him with his usual kindness, and strove to lead him into some understanding of the things belonging to his peace. The man's attention had been awakened. After leaving Godhaab he pondered over what he had heard, and could not rest satisfied without knowing more. His business carried him to a spot where the Moravian missionaries had pitched their tent

NATIVE INQUIRING OF MORAVIANS.

for the purpose of fishing; and he sought them out, as they supposed, for the sake of exchanging a portion of his provisions for some of their iron ware. But after remaining silent and thoughtful for some time, he told them that he had been with the *Pellesse* (the Greenland mode of pronouncing the Danish word *Praetz—priest* or *minister*), who

G

had told him wonderful things concerning One
who had created Heaven and earth, and whom he
called *God*. Did they know anything about it?
If they did, would they tell him; for he could not
remember all that the Pellesse had said, and he
wanted to know more. They repeated to him the
wonderful story of man's first creation in spotless
purity and perfection, the happy ruler of a world
where all things were "very good;" of his fall
into a state of sin and condemnation; of his recovery through the atonement made by a Divine
Redeemer. The stranger listened with fixed attention, remained with them the rest of the day,
was a quiet, respectful spectator of their evening
worship, and slept all night in their tent. The
thoughtful, reverent demeanour of this man, so
different from that of his countrymen generally,
made the missionaries hope that he was not far
from the kingdom of God.

In the beginning of August, 1736, just fifteen
years from the time when he had entered his
first Greenland dwelling, Mr. Egede quitted the
country which had been the scene of so many
toils and sorrows, accompanied by his daughters
and his son Niels. The storms which had assailed
them on the outward voyage were exceeded in
violence by those which they encountered on
their return, and the ship narrowly escaped the
fate of thirty others which, in one short hour,
were dashed to pieces on the coast of Norway.
Delivered from these dangers, the missionary and

his companions arrived safely at Copenhagen on
the 24th September. He was received with much
respect and sympathy by the pious members of
the Church, and by the king himself, who conferred with him about the best means of promoting
the spiritual good of the Greenlanders ; and soon
afterwards placed him in a position to carry out
his views. He was appointed superintendent of
the mission in Greenland, and empowered to
found a seminary for the education of students
and orphan youths, from amongst whom future
missionaries and catechists were to be chosen.
They were to be instructed in the Greenlandic
tongue, and in other branches of knowledge
requisite to fit them for service in that country.
In the climate of Denmark, Egede recovered in a
considerable degree his former health, and was
spared through many years of useful labour. Long
before his death the fields which he beheld so
barren were whitening to the harvest, and his
own beloved sons were not the least active and
useful among the labourers. Shortly before his
father's departure from Greenland, Paul Egede
had gone to the newly-formed station at Disko
Bay. He continued for some years in this mission,
and was greatly esteemed by the natives. He
afterwards succeeded his father in the charge of
the seminary at Copenhagen ; and employed himself in preparing various works for the assistance
of the students and missionaries, and in trans-
lating a portion of the Scriptures. Before leaving

Greenland he had translated some of the Books of Moses, but was induced to suspend the work by the representations of some Christian natives who assisted him, and who imagined that their country-men would make a bad use of some of the facts recorded in the sacred narrative; instancing, particularly, the murder of Abel by his brother Cain, the deceit of which Jacob was guilty towards his father, and various other instances of human frailty and crime which stained the lives of the patriarchs. That these worthy men, newly converted from heathen darkness, should entertain such fears, might be very natural; but it seems strange that Paul Egede should have been so much influenced by them as to withhold from the native converts the translation which he had made. We might have supposed that he who from a child had known the Scriptures would have had no fear that the study of any book in the Bible would make sin appear excusable or desir-able. He however laid aside his translation of the Old Testament, and began to translate the New, which was finished and published after his return to Denmark.

Niels Egede continued to an advanced age in the seafaring and mercantile occupations upon which he had entered in his youth; but blended with them so diligent a care for the religious instruction of the natives, that they and his own countrymen also looked upon him as being quite as much a teacher and catechist as he was a

PAUL EGEDE.

merchant and sailor. One of the first missionaries whom Mr. Egede had the happiness of sending out, was a man of remarkably devout and affectionate spirit, named Drachart. He was appointed to Godhaab, and arrived there in 1739, about a year after the beginning of that work of God which, gradually extending its gracious influence, brought a multitude of Greenlanders out of darkness into light. Drachart (whom the natives called *Pelissingoak—the little minister*, to distinguish him from one who was taller) was much beloved both by the Greenlanders and Europeans; and his preaching had a most salutary effect upon the traders and seamen employed in the service of the colony. Many who at their first coming to Greenland knew little more of the Redeemer whose name they bore than the heathen themselves, were converted to earnest Christian men by the blessing of God on his instructions; and the marked change in their conduct produced a very happy effect upon the natives who were as yet unenlightened. They perceived now that there was something in the religion preached to them which went far deeper than that outward hearing and assent, which was all they had hitherto given to it. One little incident in Drachart's missionary labours, which occurred in the third year after his coming to Greenland, may be added here. Amongst the catechumens whom he was preparing for Baptism, were two young women, whose father, when he heard that they were to be baptized, went to the missionary, and asked if he might not be baptized too? "It is true," said he, "I can say but little, and very probably I shall never learn so much as my children, for thou canst see that my hair is quite grey, and that I am a very old man; but I believe with all my heart in Jesus Christ, and that all thou sayest of Him is true." So moving a petition could not be refused, though the old man could no longer retain in his memory the catechetical instruction given to younger candidates. He was deeply affected, and the tears ran down

his cheeks like rain while Baptism was administered to himself and his children.

Sometimes the natives, coming in their accustomed wandering way of life to the Godhaab
district, and soon leaving it again, were not seen
for many years ; yet it was found that some had
carried away with them a portion at least of that
which had been taught them, and notwithstanding
the evil communications of surrounding kindred
and neighbours, they led a different life from the
heathen, and entered eternity after a different
manner. Several years after Mr. Drachart had
quitted Greenland for another field of labour, a
missionary, journeying in a distant part of the
country, came to a hut in which he found only a
sick man with his wife and two children. Making
some friendly inquiries of the poor woman about
her husband's illness, she replied, " My husband
used to put confidence in the Angekoks, but now
he minds them no more. When he is in great pain,
he says, Ah! pray to our Saviour for me. But I,
alas! can hardly pray ; I am very ignorant. Once,
indeed, I heard something from Pelissingoak, at
Godhaab, but whither is it fled !" And as she said
this she wept much. Very gladly the missionary
encouraged and comforted these poor people,
praying with them, and recalling to their memories
the instruction they had formerly received.

In 1756, King Christian VI. died, and was
succeeded by Frederic V., who continued the
favour and protection which his predecessors had

bestowed on the Greenland mission. The venerable Mr. Egede had retired from his post of superintendent some years before the death of Christian. His old age was full of peace and honour. He had taken up his abode with one of his daughters who lived in the Island of Falster; and there, on the 5th November, 1758, and in the 73rd year of his age, he departed to be with his Lord.

From the time that Egede procured the establishment of a mission in Greenland, the Danes never wholly lost sight of the country; though, as the preceding narrative has shown, the failure of their first attempts at colonization led them for a few years to abandon the settlements they had formed. Greenland has now long been wholly a Danish colony; about a thousand Danes residing at various points of the coast, to manage the trade with the mother-country, which consists chiefly in the exchange of European articles for oil, and skins of seals, reindeer, &c. The Greenlanders, or Esquimaux (as they are now generally called), are not subject to the Danish laws, but they are much attached to the Danes, and wholly under their influence. A clergyman, a doctor, and a schoolmaster, whose duty it is to give gratuitous instruction and relief to the natives, are stationed in each district, and paid by the government. All the people of West Greenland have become Christians, and many are able to read and write.

MATTHEW STACH AND HIS ASSOCIATES;

THE FOUNDERS OF THE MORAVIAN MISSIONS IN GREENLAND AND LABRADOR.

AT the beginning of the eighteenth century, a few descendants from the ancient Unitas Fratrum still lingered in Moravia, amongst whom were the parents of the missionary brethren whose labours form the chief subjects of the following pages. Sheltered in some degree from persecution by their poverty and obscure condition, they were nevertheless exposed from time to time to the operation of penal statutes, which were made to bear more or less hardly upon them, according to the inclination of the reigning emperor, or the political circumstances of the times. The public exercise of their worship had long been prohibited; neither might they safely allow it to be known that they possessed any other than the Roman Catholic version of the Scriptures, or any copies of their liturgy, or other religious works. The forefathers of Matthew Stach and his brethren had been all subjected to exile, imprisonment, torture, and death itself, for their profession of the faith; which they claimed to have preserved (though not always in equal purity), ever since the Gospel had been introduced into their country, by missionaries of the Greek church, in the course of the ninth century. But under the silence and concealment which persecution had compelled their descendants to observe, with regard to their religious doctrines, many, especially of the younger people, were in danger of losing their faith altogether. To obviate this evil, a few zealous men began to act as missionaries to their brethren, travelling up and down in the districts where they chiefly resided, to exhort them not to swerve from the faith for which their predecessors had suffered so severely, and endeavouring, above all, to awaken in them a spirit of greater earnestness and devotion. Nor were their labours unfruitful. At the end of a few years, a powerful religious movement began to make itself felt among the brethren in Moravia. But the harsh treatment to which they were always liable, and which at this time was inflicted upon some of their number, caused many to long for a retreat where they might serve God in peace, and revive the religious discipline and ritual of their ancestors.

Having heard that there was greater liberty of conscience in Saxony and Silesia, many sought an asylum in those countries. A small body, who emigrated in 1722, were kindly received in Lusatia (a territory lying between the two above-named countries), where Count Zinzendorf, the owner of the estate of Bertholsdorf, encouraged them to settle on his land. Accordingly, on a hill called Hutberg, they erected a small village,

HERRNHUT IN MORAVIA.

which they named Herrnhut (the Lord's Watch.) The leader of this little band was a man of much energy and piety, named Christian David. Having found so secure an asylum for his people, he ventured repeatedly to return to Moravia, for the purpose of guiding and encouraging other emigrants to escape thither; since the severity with which their rulers prohibited emigration, rendered the enterprise difficult and hazardous. Many were arrested ere they had crossed the frontier, and punished by scourging and imprisonment; but at the end of ten years, the population of the colony at Herrnhut amounted to six hundred persons, and it was at this time that the brethren entered upon their first missionary undertakings. A few words concerning the early life of the chief Greenland missionaries, Matthew Stach, Frederic Bœhnisch, and John Beck, may fitly precede the history of their mission.

In the great persecution of 1620, the ancestors of Matthew Stach were compelled to quit their native land, and flee into Saxony. Many years afterwards, some of their descendants ventured back to Moravia, amongst whom was Christian Stach, the father of Matthew. He was a man of exemplary life, so much esteemed by his neighbours for his meek and benevolent disposition, that, although stigmatized as a heretic, and known to be warmly attached to his religion, he remained during several years almost unmolested. Christian Stach bent all his efforts to train up his children in the fear of God. " The first time," said Matthew, " that I ever had any serious thoughts, they arose in this way. When I was about four or five years old, my father one day found me crying bitterly because, in the general distribution of the cake, a very small slice had fallen to my share. He gave me a larger piece, saying, at the same time, ' My child, if thou wouldst thus weep over thy sins, it were better.' These words sank into my heart." In his sixth year the little boy began to herd the cattle in summer time, but in the winter was carefully instructed by his father; who was well read in the Scriptures and in the writings of the Reformers, though he had had little opportunity of acquiring secular learning. "My father," writes Matthew, "took particular pains to teach me to pray, often telling me what I should ask of my Father in Heaven. In my childish days, I was much concerned about the salvation of my soul, and often very unhappy because I could not feel that God was well-pleased with me. But going from home at twelve years of age, to enter into service, these serious thoughts were almost banished by new scenes and occupations. I now made many acquaintances of my own age, and would gladly have shared in their pastimes; but for the most part they rejected my company, and treated me with contumely, because I was, said they, '*a heretic.*' In my next situation, I met with more friendly comrades, and enjoyed much more liberty. My master was, however, a pious man, who failed not to admonish me when he saw that I was turning aside to evil; but I had become too fond of company, and eager for amusement; and though conscience reproached me for running into temptation, I often joined the band of men and boys who frequented the village tavern to drink, dance, and divert themselves."

In the course of a year or two, however, all his early religious impressions were revived in full force. " My master," he says, " had been speaking to me very seriously on the course of life I was leading. His words went to my heart, as those of my father had done, twelve years before; and a voice in my inmost soul said, *Thou must pray.* I did so, and from that time never again suffered the day to pass by without prayer." Even in his most careless days, Matthew Stach had sometimes longed that he and his kindred could escape from the severe restraint in which they were held by their popish rulers, to some spot where they might worship God after the manner of their forefathers. The wish now acquired fresh force, and, hearing the settlement at Herrnhut spoken of, he resolved to go thither whatever difficulties might beset his way. But his father did not at first approve of this scheme. " I have long toiled for your benefit, my son," said he, "and I hoped that now you would soon be able to take my place, and become the stay and comfort of your mother and sisters." Matthew loved his parents too sincerely to oppose his own wishes to theirs. The father, however, perceiving that his son continued somewhat sad and anxious, said to him, " My dear son, if you think that you cannot serve God faithfully in this land, and are really animated by the desire to do His will and save your soul, go to Herrnhut. I would not for the whole world keep you back." Upon this Matthew set out with a glad heart, but secretly, and by night. He gained the frontier without accident, and in due time arrived safely at Herrnhut, but with only a few pence in his pocket. At first, he could hardly, by the most diligent labour, gain a sufficient quantity of the necessaries of life. This, however, was a small trouble, compared with the sorrow occasioned by sad tidings from home. A cousin of Matthew's had joined him at Herrnhut, and the fathers of both the young men had been severely punished for the flight of their sons; laid in irons, and sentenced to hard labour. The father of Matthew was released after a short captivity, but his uncle remained a prisoner almost to the day of his death. The two youths set out again for Moravia, determined to effect the escape of their relatives, if possible ; and although they could not at that time accomplish their purpose, all the surviving members of the family were eventually reunited at Herrnhut; but in deep poverty, for they had been obliged to leave all their goods behind them.

His chief earthly wish was thus fulfilled, yet Matthew Stach was still far from peace. Notwithstanding his religious education, his eyes were not yet opened to see clearly the true meaning of the Gospel, and he was labouring to obtain repose of mind by his own righteousness. His anxiety was aggravated by a mistaken notion which prevailed amongst his brethren at that time, that a Christian must necessarily enjoy the full assurance that his sins are forgiven. To obtain this, he fasted, and watched, and prayed whole nights through, till his strength gave way. Reduced now almost to despair, he cried out, " Ah Lord, take pity on me, I am lost!" "But," said he, " in this time of utter distress, the Friend who had sought and found me, though I dared not believe it, drew near to my soul, and my ears were opened to hear His voice, saying, Peace be unto thee. From that time I walked in peace, and gave thanks to God in my heart continually, though I said nothing to any man of my great happiness."

Frederic Bœhnisch was the son of a miller at Kunewald, in Moravia. Like Matthew Stach, he enjoyed the blessings of a good example and a religious education in his father's house. Although forbidden the public exercises of Divine worship according to the manner which their consciences approved, so that they could participate in no other services than those of the Roman Catholic church, the parents of Frederic Bœhnisch, and a few of their neighbours who held the same faith as themselves, were accustomed to meet secretly, from time to time, to join in the prayers and hymns hallowed by the memory of pious forefathers, and endeared to the Unitas Fratrum by centuries of persecution. At these meetings the Scriptures were read and explained, according to their ability, by some of the brethren who have already been described as acting the part of missionaries among their dispersed fellow-religionists. When Frederic was about twelve years old, he was per-

mitted for the first time to attend one of these
meetings, and was so deeply moved by the prayers
and exhortations which he heard there, that the
impression was never effaced from his mind.
From that day he resolved that, as soon as the
opportunity should be granted him, he would
leave his native place, and seek out some spot
where with his fellow-believers he might worship
God openly, and as frequently as he would. "I
asked," he says, "where such a place could be
found, and the answer was, 'In Saxony, which
lies towards the west.' After that, I went every
day into our garden, and kneeling down with my
face towards the west, prayed earnestly, and often
with tears, that God would bring me to that
place." Two years had passed away when one of
the missionary brethren, whose words had so
deeply moved the heart of Frederic, came again
to Kunewald. He was about to visit other places
where families of the brethren lived, dispersed
amidst the Roman Catholic population. The lad
besought permission to accompany him; but he
was as yet too young for full reliance to be placed
on his stedfastness and discretion; and his father,
knowing from experience how closely the move-
ments of the brethren were watched, and fearing
lest his son might by any means bring their friend
into trouble, would not consent to his going.

Shortly afterwards, however, tidings of the
infant colony which had just been planted at
Bertholsdorf, reached the dwellers at Kunewald.

A little company, one of whom was a near kins-man of Bœhnisch's, determined to migrate thither, if possible; and Frederic entreated that he might go with them so earnestly, that his father and mother were induced to consent. "We set off," he says, "on Palm Sunday, after night-fall, and by Easter-day had reached in safety a town where Protestants were allowed to celebrate their public worship. Here for the first time in my life I heard a sermon from a pastor of the Reformed Church. On the following Sunday, we came in sight of Bertholsdorf. Only three houses had yet been erected on the Hutberg, and these were not finished. But my heart overflowed with joy and gratitude, for God had granted my petition and brought me to dwell amongst brethren." The strength and sincerity of the boy's religious principles were now to be tested by trial. He had left the homely plenty and comfort of his father's house to cast in his lot with a very poor people, but he never repented of his choice. Working at any occupation which he could find, sometimes as a linen weaver, sometimes as a gardener, he was contented and happy with the hardest fare. He had been living at Herrnhut between three and four years when Matthew Stach arrived there; they were nearly of the same age, and a warm friendship soon sprang up between them.

The family of John Beck had suffered with peculiar severity for their adherence to their faith. His grandfather, crippled by the tortures inflicted on him, died young, leaving two sons who were taken from their mother to be brought up as Roman Catholics. But in the mind of the elder boy the instructions of his parents had taken root too deeply to be eradicated. The fruit of them appeared in the diligence with which in after-life he searched the Scriptures, and sought out amongst his neighbours all who had any desire to serve God, that he might persuade them to join with him in the pursuit of sacred knowledge, and other works of piety. More particularly he took pains to instruct his little son John in the word of God. When the boy was old enough to enter into the service of strangers, his father dismissed him with these words: "My son, have the blessed God always before thy eyes, so shall it be well with thee, in time and eternity." "And for a time," said John Beck, "I laid this injunction much to heart; though, by degrees, I forgot it, and became very indifferent about pleasing God. One day, however, while about my master's work, I happened to look into a New Testament, and lighted upon these words, 'I know thy works, that thou art neither cold nor hot.' I read the verses which follow, and the words were like fire, they pierced my very heart." This proved the turning point in the life of John Beck. The shame and sorrow with which he was filled, on account of his lukewarmness and ingratitude towards the Saviour, were succeeded by a lively

faith in the atonement. "I saw Him," he says,
"as it were crucified before me, and for my sins,
and was filled with inexpressible thankfulness
and desire to glorify Him."

The change which had passed upon the young
man quickly attracted the observation of his comrades, to whom, indeed, he spoke freely, warning,
and entreating them to turn with their hearts to
the Lord. Some were gained by his exhortations,
and in their turn began to speak of the Gospel
among their neighbours. In course of time, many
were awakened to consider more seriously the
things that belonged to their peace; and began
to meet together to pray and read the Scriptures.
Amongst their neighbours, some approved, others
derided this new zeal for religion; but the authorities of the neighbourhood were deeply offended, and put an end to the meetings by arresting
John Beck and another young man who had taken
a prominent part in them. The two young men
were sentenced to be separately confined in irons,
and to be fed on just so much bread and water
as was necessary to keep them alive. Beck, in
particular, was most severely handled, but he
received grace to be stedfast, and has left it on
record, that the abiding consciousness of God's
presence made his prison seem like a home to
him. When their captivity had lasted some time,
Beck's fellow-prisoner obtained a little indulgence
from his gaoler, and was even permitted to walk
about a little within the gaol. He made use of his

liberty to visit the cell where his friend was lying in fetters, and together they found means to concert a plan of escape, as well as to loosen the irons. They scaled the walls of the prison successfully, but their flight was discovered before they had got half a mile from the town. Though hotly pursued, however, they contrived to creep into the thickets and hide themselves, and, in the end, made good their escape. Having neither money nor food, they begged their way towards Breslau, where one of them had some Lutheran acquaintances, amongst whom they hoped to find shelter. But while they were still far from that town, a poor farmer, struck with pity at their famished way-worn appearance, took them to his house, and charitably entertained them for some days. Finding that they were refugees from Moravia, he spoke to them of Herrnhut. It was the first time they had heard of the settlement formed there, but they at once resolved to go thither rather than to Breslau; and after encountering many more hardships, arrived safely at the asylum of their brethren, in the summer of 1732.

Count Zinzendorf, the benevolent benefactor of the community at Herrnhut, had already begun to direct their attention to the deplorable state of the heathen world. An earnest desire to be instrumental in spreading the word of life among pagan nations had taken possession of his mind during his studies at the university, but was not called into exercise until the year 1731, when he attended the coronation of Christian VI. at Copenhagen. In that city he met with two Greenlanders who had been baptized by the venerable Mr. Egede, and learned with pain that the mission to Greenland was to be relinquished. His domestics also conversed with a baptized negro from St. Thomas, who earnestly entreated that Christian missionaries might be sent to his enslaved countrymen. He appeared deeply interested in the fate of his sister, whom he had left behind in that island, and who, he said, frequently besought the great God to send some one who might show her the way to Him. The count afforded him an opportunity of stating his case in a public meeting of the brethren at Herrnhut, where his representations and entreaties proved so effectual, that two of those present, Leonard Dober and another, offered to go to St. Thomas, though under the persuasion that they would be obliged to sell themselves for slaves in order to gain access to the negroes. They set sail August 21st, 1732, ten years after the foundation of Herrnhut.

At the same time the plan of a mission to Greenland was also agitated. As that country was under the protection of the Danish government, which was very friendly to the brethren, it appeared the more eligible for the establishment of a mission. Matthew Stach and Frederic Boehnisch, had both, unknown to each other, formed the design of offering themselves for this service.

After a minute inquiry into their motives for such an undertaking, the offer was accepted, but the mission to St. Thomas having exhausted the resources of the little community for that year, the commencement of the Greenland mission was deferred until January, 1733. In the mean time Frederic Bœhnisch had been despatched on a long journey to transact some business for his brethren, and in his absence, Christian Stach consented to accompany his cousin Matthew. Christian David went with them, on account of their youth and inexperience, intending to return to Europe, as soon as he had seen the mission fairly established. With scarcely any provision for their journey beyond the most necessary articles of clothing, our missionaries travelled by way of Hamburgh to the Danish capital. Here they met with a kind reception from Professor Ewald, member of the College of Missions, and other friends to whom they had been recommended. Their intention of going to Greenland was, however, regarded as a visionary scheme, particularly while the fate of the Danish mission at Godhaab was yet in suspense. But they took little notice of the gloomy forebodings which met their ears, believing that He who had called them to the work, would support them in the prosecution of it. They learned shortly after that his majesty had granted leave for one more vessel to sail to Godhaab, and applied to the king's chamberlain for permission to take their passage in her.

Their first audience of this minister was not a little discouraging. Indeed, it might well seem strange to him that young men, who possessed no advantages of study or experience, should hope to succeed, where the indefatigable exertions of the pious and learned Egede had accomplished so little. But being convinced, by a closer acquaintance, of the solidity of their faith, and the rectitude of their intentions, he became their firm friend, willingly presented their memorial to the king, and exerted all his influence in their behalf; making use, it is said, of this argument, that God hath, in all ages, employed things which are weak, unlearned, and of no account, in the world's estimation, as instruments in the accomplishment of His great designs, in order that man might ascribe the honour to Him alone, and not rely on his own power and sagacity. The king, moved by the representations of his minister, consented to their request, and wrote with his own hand a recommendatory letter to Mr. Egede. The chamberlain also introduced them to several persons distinguished by their rank and piety, who generously contributed towards the expense of their voyage and intended settlement. Being asked one day how they proposed to maintain themselves in Greenland, they answered that they depended on the labour of their own hands and God's blessing; and that, not to be burdensome to any one, they would build themselves a house and cultivate the ground. It being objected that they would find no wood to build with, as the country presented little but a face of barren rock ; " Then," replied they, " we will dig into the earth and lodge there." " No," said the chamberlain, "you shall not be reduced to that necessity. Here are fifty dollars ; buy timber, and take it out with you." With this and other donations, they purchased poles, planks, and laths; instruments for agriculture, masonry, and carpenter's work ; several sorts of seeds and roots; implements of fishing and hunting; household furniture, books, paper, and provisions.

Thus equipped they took a grateful leave of the court where they had been so hospitably entertained, and embarked on board the king's ship Caritas, on the 10th April. The congregation at Herrnhut had adopted the custom of annually compiling a collection of Scripture texts for every day in the year. This text was called the *Daily Word ;* it supplied a subject for private meditation and a theme for the public discourses. It was long remembered by the brethren that the Daily Word for that 10th of April, when their missionaries embarked upon an undertaking which so often appeared to baffle all hope, was (Heb. xi. 1), " Faith is the substance of things hoped for, the evidence of things not seen." In that faith they set sail, nor were they confounded by the unspeakable difficulties of following years, until, at last, they and their brethren in Europe beheld the fulfilment of their hopes. On the

thirty-third day of the voyage they came in sight
of the coast of Greenland, but a violent tempest of
four days' continuance, preceded by a total eclipse
of the sun, drove them back sixty leagues. On the
20th May, they cast anchor in Baal's River, and
joyfully welcomed the snowy cliffs and savage inhabitants of a country which had so long been the
chief subject of their thoughts.

Immediately on landing they repaired to Mr.
Egede, who received them with a cordial welcome, and confirmed their hope that, dark as
was the present aspect of affairs, the light of
the Lord should yet dawn upon Greenland.
Their first care was to find a spot on which to
plant their intended habitation. They selected
a piece of ground between the harbour and the
factory or village of Godhaab, on the south-west
side of a small peninsula, the outermost edge of
which formed three strands, between which the
rocks projected into the sea. Between the rocks
the beach was fenced with a dam of pebbles
thrown up by the waves. It rose with a gradual
acclivity, and ended in a small valley watered by
a rivulet. Here, about a mile distant from the
edge of the sea, they determined to fix their
abode, and as the erection of the house, for which
their friends in Denmark had presented them
with timber, would be a work of time, they
raised a hut of turf and stones, Greenland fashion,
to shelter them during its progress. It was
now June, yet the weather was so piercingly

cold that the sods froze in their hands while they
built.

In the middle of the month the Caritas sailed
on her homeward voyage. From the letters
which Matthew Stach sent by it to the congregation at Herrnhut, a few passages are here
extracted. " Brethren and sisters, beloved in
Jesus, through whose grace we have life: God
who is rich in loving-kindness has brought us in
peace to this land. That which we sought we
have found; a people knowing nothing of their
Maker. They care for nothing excepting to catch
seals, fish, and reindeer, and in quest of these they
wander up and down continually. We long to
learn their language and tell them of God, of His
Son Jesus, of the Holy Spirit; we long to seek
them out and make them our friends, but know
not how to come at them, for to-day they are here,
to-morrow there; on the islands, on the shores,
away beyond our reach. Did we foresee how
many difficulties would obstruct this undertaking
when, at Herrnhut, we resolved to attempt it?
To that question I answer, there is a true saying,
' The man who keeps his faith cannot lose his
way.' Our way is shut up, so that we see it not.
But it is our daily lesson, To be still in the Lord.
All is well with us outwardly, but our hearts long
to win souls, and towards this we can as yet do
nothing. By the grace of God, we will not
despond, but watch for the Lord. When His
time comes to favour this land, its darkness shall

be turned into light, and the ice-cold hearts of its people shall be thawed. While our way is upright before Him, we are not troubled though men esteem us fools, and truly we are fools in the eyes of many who know this land and its inhabitants."

To the young men who had been more especially his companions, he writes: "I address you, my brethren, from a land where the Name of Jesus is not yet known. Here the Sun of Righteousness has not shined, but you live in the light of His meridian beams. Has He yet warmed your hearts? or are some of you still frozen? It were better to have lived in Greenland and never heard of Jesus, than to have the light shining all around you, and yet not to arise and walk as children of the light. But you who have known the Saviour, may you be established in grace. My heart is listed with yours under the banner of the cross. To Christ will I live, to Him will I die. Let us animate each other to follow the Lamb without the camp. The salvation is great, and the harvest will be glorious, when we have sown much seed and watered it with many tears. Remember your meanest brother constantly in your prayers."

All the honest warmth and confidence expressed by the writer were needed to sustain himself and his brother missionaries under the various difficulties which lay before them, and which were greater in some respects than those which had obstructed the labours of Egede. It was necessary, in order to the very existence of their mission, that they should toil much, both with head and hand in occupations which were new to them. Natives of a country which lay remote from the sea, they were totally inexperienced in navigation. Nor were they much better acquainted with the arts of the fisher and fowler. Now, however, fish, birds, and reindeer must be caught, to eke out their slender stock of European provisions; and drift-wood must be gathered on the shores and islands during the summer months, to provide firing for the long Arctic winter. The missionaries had purchased an old boat from the captain of the Caritas, and whenever the weather would permit, they went out in search of food or fuel. But, as may easily be imagined, they encountered many dangers and endured many hungry days of disappointed labour, before they learnt how to manage a boat in those stormy ice-encumbered seas; or became sufficiently expert in hunting and fishing to obtain an adequate supply of food. They were the more desirous to acquire some skill in navigation, because it was only by means of boat voyages that they could hope to become acquainted with a wandering people, scattered along the shores of a hundred creeks and fiords. These occupations, however, needful and onerous as they were, did not cause them so many anxious thoughts as the study of the native language. Mr. Egede kindly put into their hands the grammar and vocabulary and other papers which he had drawn up, that they might make copies of these manuscripts for themselves; and his sons frequently assisted their studies by explaining the grammatical rules and remarks which their father had written down. But when it is remembered that Matthew Stach and his associates had never before seen a grammar, and knew not the meaning of the terms employed; and moreover that they were obliged to learn Danish before they could understand their instructors; it will not be thought wonderful, that the difficulties which had proved formidable to Egede appeared to these unlearned students to be almost insurmountable.

Christian David was too old to engage in the study of the language with any hope of success. He occupied himself with matters of household economy, and with the building of the mission dwelling, which was sufficiently advanced to be habitable before the winter set in. The hut which had hitherto served the brethren for a home, was preserved, in hope that by the time they had acquired a sufficient knowledge of Greenlandic to converse with the natives, inquirers would often visit the station, to whom the hut might afford a temporary shelter, if the missionaries could persuade them to remain a while. The mission-house contained, besides the necessary rooms for the brethren a larger apartment designed to be used as a chapel and schoolroom; and ardently the young men hoped and longed to see it filled with native scholars and worshippers. Christian David sympathized in their desire, but was far less sanguine in hope. "I built the first dwelling for the missionaries, and the first school-house for the natives," he said, when better days had come, "but little expected that the dwelling would continue to be inhabited, or that the school-room would ever become too small." At present, the station which the missionaries, in remembrance of their German home, called New Herrnhut, was visited not unfrequently by a few natives, but they came only to beg or to purloin such articles as suited their fancy, and, as if inspired by the very spirit of mischief, they stole away the manuscripts on which their hosts were bestowing so much labour. Both house and hut, however, were soon to be filled even to crowding, but it was with sick and dying sufferers, not with scholars in the Word of God.

The first and most terrible outbreak of small-pox in Greenland, and the manner in which the country round Godhaab was depopulated by it, have been described in the memoir of Egede. Following the example of that venerable man, the Moravian brethren went from place to place to visit and succour the sick, many of whom they received and nursed under their own roof. There were very few instances in which the

care bestowed on the sufferers was rewarded
by their recovery, and of all those who caught
the fatal infection, scarcely one in a hundred
survived. From nurses, the brethren became
patients. Their health had been much impaired
by the fatigue and other distressing circumstances which attended their care of the sick,
and as winter advanced the extreme cold caused
them to be attacked with scurvy, so that they
could at times hardly move their limbs. But
they accounted it a great instance of God's
merciful care over them that they were never
all three reduced to helplessness at the same
time. Each in his turn was able to wait upon
the others. In these scenes of sickness and sorrow the winter months passed away. When spring
returned, the invaluable scurvy-grass, which had
shot up plentifully beneath the snow, proved
an effectual remedy for the disorder of the
missionaries. But the small-pox lingered among
the natives far into the summer, and for many
leagues around Godhaab and New Herrnhut,
the land was without inhabitants. When the
Danish factors made their customary trading
voyages they found only empty huts, and un-
buried corpses, often half devoured by foxes
and ravens. And at the various sealing and
fishing stations, to which, at that time of year,
numerous companies of Greenlanders from distant
places usually resorted, not a tent was to be seen
on the shore, or a kayak upon the waters. The

natives shunned all that coast, and the islands which lay near it, as the nest of the plague.

Christian David, and Christian Stach, seeing that the country had thus become a mere wilderness, thought it would be useless to remain, and resolved to take the first opportunity of returning to Europe, and seeking a more promising field of labour. But Matthew Stach, notwithstanding all discouragements, was determined not to abandon his post, even though long years of disappointed hope should be his portion, as they had been that of Egede. And before his companions could put their resolution to quit the country into effect, their drooping hearts were cheered by the arrival of fresh labourers. The king of Denmark had expressed a wish that the number of missionaries from Herrnhut might be increased. Accordingly, John Beck and Frederic Bœhnisch were chosen, and willingly undertook this work. They repaired first to Berlin, where Dr. Jablonsky, a senior, or bishop of the United Brethren, who was also the king's chaplain, received them with much kindness, and set them forward on their way with prayer. At Copenhagen, where they were detained two months, they found a good friend in Baron von Sœlenthal, Governor of the Crown Prince. Through his interposition they obtained a passage to Greenland, free of expense, in a ship which was proceeding thither, laden with materials for the erection of a new colony at Disko. He pre-

I

sented them also with a quantity of meal, and other articles of food necessary for their support. A portion of these valuable stores they took with them; but there being very little room on board the ship, they were obliged to leave the remainder to be forwarded by another vessel. Now began their first experience of the outward trials of missionary life. The friendly feeling which had been manifested towards them in Copenhagen had no existence on board the ship; and their voyage, though less tempestuous than that of their predecessors, was rendered very painful by the mockeries, abusive language, and hard treatment which were their daily portion. Glad indeed were they when the friendly countenance of Christian David greeted them at Disko. The vessel which preceded theirs had put in at Godhaab, and brought tidings of the new settlement about to be founded, and Christian David had been engaged to assist in the erection of the buildings. To this good work Beck and Bœhnisch also lent a hand; till the ship sailed again for Godhaab, where their arrival caused great joy to the Stachs, and dispelled all Christian's desire to quit the country.

Encouraging one another to pray and labour, the missionaries diligently pursued their outdoor occupations and their study of the language. By practice they became tolerably skilful fishermen, and supplied themselves with food; and notwithstanding several misadventures from stormy

weather, they visited various parts of the coast,
and increased their knowledge of the country and
its inhabitants. But their longest voyages, one of
which extended one hundred miles to the south,
and another an equal distance northwards, were
undertaken in company of the traders, to whom
their assistance was not unwelcome in a perilous
navigation, attended with storms of rain and snow,
and contrary winds. The natives whom they met
with in these distant excursions appeared more
inclined to welcome their visits than any with
whom they had yet made acquaintance. At first,
seeing that the missionaries assisted readily in
every kind of manual labour, the Greenlanders
supposed that they were the factor's servants, and
treated them with contempt; but finding that this
was not the case, and observing the gentle friendly
demeanour of the strangers, the natives invited
them to come into their tents, and sought to converse with them. Without an interpreter neither
party was very intelligible to the other, yet the
people were pleased; they desired the missionaries to repeat their visit another year, and promised to return it when, in the course of their
journeyings, they came into the neighbourhood of
Godhaab. These expressions of goodwill cheered
the brethren in their application to the language,
which they still found full of difficulties. The
pronunciation, the numerous affixes and inflections,
the great variety of words expressive of common
objects and ideas, so that the slightest shades of

difference in a thing were distinguished by appropriate terms, all these required long patience, and the practice of years. They received valuable help at this time from Paul Egede, who had lately returned from Denmark. He set apart time every week for teaching them to speak and translate; and it was not long before they found themselves able to talk about the common objects and affairs of life with sufficient accuracy to be easily understood by the natives.

When the brethren attempted to enter upon religious subjects, they discovered, as Mr. Egede had done before them, that it was hardly possible to find appropriate words by which to express their meaning. They wisely resolved to refrain from speaking upon sacred things, until they were better acquainted with the language, lest they should confuse the minds of the natives, and expose the Christian doctrine to ridicule, by the employment of incongruous or equivocal words. Notwithstanding their adherence to this rule, some misunderstandings arose. For instance, a curious misconception was caused by their use of the Danish word *Gud*, which signifies God. When the brethren began to speak to the Greenlanders of the Almighty Creator of all things, not knowing by what native word to express with sufficient solemnity the name of the Divine Being, they had recourse to the Danish *Gud*, which was likely to be already known to some of the people through their frequent intercourse with the Danes. But the missionaries did not know that the Greenlandic possessed a word precisely similar in sound, signifying *rivers*. They learnt afterwards that many of the natives were much astonished that the strangers should speak so earnestly about the existence of rivers, which no one ever doubted; and one man being asked if he believed in *Gud*, answered, indignantly, "Why should I not believe in *that?* I have heard its voice;" meaning the roar of the torrents which gush from the glaciers. While unable to *speak* on religious subjects, the brethren took such opportunities as they could find, of reading to the people portions of Scripture, short prayers, etc., which Mr. Egede had translated. One day, when Matthew Stach had been reading a prayer to a party of natives, they told him that he had spoken good Greenlandic, but added, " We do not understand what you mean; 'Being redeemed by the blood of Jesus Christ,' ' knowing Christ,'—this language is too high to enter into our ears."

Two years had now elapsed since the terrible visitation of small-pox, and the natives no longer shunned the neighbourhood of Baal's River. The people frequenting the fishing stations near Godhaab paid frequent visits to New Herrnhut. Some came to ask for food, some for a night's lodging, others for knives, needles, fish-hooks, etc.; not one in fifty had any higher motive for resorting to the mission-house than curiosity, or the hope of gain. Some of them, indeed, openly declared, that

if the missionaries did not continue to give them
stock-fish, they would no longer listen to their
words. But selfish, and thievish also, as were
most of their visitors, the missionaries would not
drive them away. By persevering kindness they
hoped to win, sooner or later, some of these people
to better things; and they were pleased to see
that a few who had remained with them till the
hour of their evening worship, and had witnessed
their meeting for prayer and psalmody, seemed to
be unusually interested, begged permission to
come again, and asked many questions as to the
intention of the missionaries, desiring to know
why they knelt down? to whom they spoke, &c.,
&c. Besides their daily meetings for prayer, the
brethren set apart an hour every evening for conversing together respecting their mission, and
communicating the various difficulties, hopes, and
apprehensions which the subject suggested to their
minds, that each might profit by the experience of
all. And that nothing might prevent the closest
union between them, as brothers engaged in one
common work, they resolved each to examine himself—whether he believed that his call to this
mission was of God, and was resolved never to
abandon it, what trials soever he might have to
endure, until he could conscientiously say that he
had fulfilled his duty as a faithful servant to the
utmost possible extent; or until God, in His providence, should remove him from this field of
labour? They revolved these questions in their

minds during some weeks before they communicated to one another the results of their self-
inquiry.

It then appeared that Christian Stach had never
considered himself bound to devote the whole of
his life to the service of the heathen; he had
rather undertaken the voyage to Greenland upon
trial, and to supply the place of an absent
brother. Nevertheless he would remain in his
present position till God should remove him, or
till called away by the congregation of the brethren in Europe. Christian David had been sent
to Greenland, for the purpose of aiding his two
young inexperienced brethren to lay the foundation of a mission settlement; and as this had now
been done, he intended the next summer to return to Herrnhut, and again place his services at
the disposal of the brethren there. Soon afterwards he took his departure, not without the promise that the Greenland mission should have a
chief place in his prayers, as well as every service
which he could render it by his exertions in
Europe. Matthew Stach, Frederic Bœhnisch, and
John Beck had given themselves to the mission,
for life or for death, resolving to believe where
they could not see, and to hope even against hope.
Nor would they relinquish their enterprise, till
they could appeal to God, with the testimony of
their conscience, that they had done all that man
could do. And they bound themselves at this
time by a solemn agreement: 1. To keep in

mind that they had come to that country, resting themselves upon God their Saviour, in whom all the nations of the earth shall be blessed. 2. To labour both by word and deed, as God should give them ability, to make known that Jesus hath redeemed mankind by the shedding of His own blood; that by this doctrine tho hearts of the heathen might be brought to the obedience of faith. 3. To dwell together in brotherly love, each acknowledging the spiritual gifts bestowed by God upon his brethren, in honour preferring one another. 4. To perform their various secular labours diligently and heartily, as unto the Lord, but not to give way to anxious thoughts about the supply of their temporal wants, casting their cares upon Him who feeds the sparrows and clothes the flowers of the field. They sealed this agreement by partaking together of the Lord's Supper.

Soon did the missionaries need all the comfort that could be derived from their consciousness of unanimity, for the sincerity and strength of their faith was about to be severely tested. The liberality with which an eminent benefactor at the Danish court provided for the supply of their wants in a former year has been mentioned. Since that time no provisions had reached them. Even the stores which Frederic Bœhnisch and John Beck had left behind, were forgotten by the persons who should have forwarded them, and were never sent to Greenland. The fishing and hunting seasons of 1735 had been extremely unfavourable; there was a general scarcity of food in the colony, and the missionaries had been unable to lay up any stock of fish or reindeer's flesh. Their salted provisions were exhausted, and nothing remained to them but a very small quantity of meal and pease, and a few ship biscuits. Christian David, who was now on his voyage home, would make known their need to the brethren at Herrnhut; but winter was close at hand, and many months must necessarily elapse before any ships would reach the colony. The Danish settlers compassionated their distress, but were powerless to relieve it, being themselves straitened for provisions.

The only resource left to the brethren was to purchase seals' flesh from the Greenlanders, if they could prevail on them to part with any. For none of the Europeans were at all expert at catching these creatures; only the natives, in their kayaks, which they managed with inimitable dexterity, were successful in the seal-hunt. But the Greenlanders were most unwilling to part with any portion of their spoils; and even the men who, during a former winter, had been most liberally relieved by the bounty of the missionaries, refused now to sell them a morsel of food at any price. In extenuation of this ungrateful selfishness, it must be remembered that the natives ordinarily passed their lives (and especially during the winter) in alternate fasting and feasting.

When provisions were plentiful, the people would
prolong their repasts through whole nights, gorg-
ing themselves to a degree which appeared in-
comprehensible to Europeans.   But when tem-

SEAL-FISHING IN GREENLAND.

pestuous weather, or excessive accumulations of
ice, prevented them from obtaining seals, or other
food, they were forced to sustain life, for days and
weeks together, by eating seaweed, the leather of
their boots, old tent skins, &c., &c. Nor was there
a year in which many persons did not die of want.
The brethren now esteemed themselves happy if
they could find a sufficiency of mussels and sea-
weed to allay the pangs of hunger. The small

remnant of their meal they eked out, as far as possible, by boiling it with some of their old tallow candles; and revolting as this mess would have seemed to them but a few weeks before, they were thankful for it now. In the extreme cold of the Arctic regions, some portion of animal fat or oil, however coarse its nature, appears absolutely necessary to sustain man's life.

They encountered many perils in searching for food. Their boat was so worn out that it was hardly fit for use, even in the calmest weather, but the urgency of their need compelled them to venture out in it. One day when they were returning home, and had nearly reached the shore, a sudden squall drove them back several miles, and obliged them to take refuge on a rocky island, where, the wind continuing contrary, they were forced to remain four nights, wet to the skin with rain and spray. Another time, their strength failing them after long plying at the oar, they halted for the night at an uninhabited spot, which afforded them no other shelter than a hole which they dug out in the snow, and in which they lay down till they were sufficiently rested to keep themselves warm by running. Happily for them, it was yet too early for the extreme cold of winter. The natives who witnessed the poverty and privations of the brethren, were astonished that they should choose to live at a distance from their own country, in so mean and miserable a condition, and were not sparing in their expressions of contempt for this folly, as it appeared to them. "Your countrymen," they would often say, "must be worthless people, since they send you nothing, and you will be fools if you stay here." In all this time of adversity, the hope and fortitude of the brethren were sustained by the belief that their heavenly Father would not forsake them. "We know not," they wrote in their journal, "what He intends to do with us. We can only observe that other trials await us. As little do we comprehend what His secret hand has been doing among the heathen. Gross darkness appears still to cover their hearts and minds. Yet we believe that at length the work shall prosper; and when He has tried and proved us, He will not fail to let us see His glory."

Many instances of God's providential care are gratefully recorded in the journals of the mission. For example, the finding of a dead "white whale," which the missionaries and the boatmen of the Danish settlement shared between them, and found the flesh "red like beef, and not unlike it in flavour." The gift of a young porpoise, bestowed on them by a Greenlander who had caught the dam. The being driven by a contrary wind to some rocks where they espied an eagle sitting upon its nest, shot it, and having with some difficulty clambered up, found four large eggs, as well as the dead bird, which, besides food, supplied them with quills, an article of which they were greatly in want. But more than by all these

reliefs and alleviations, their distress was miti-
gated, and their hearts were comforted, by the
seasonable kindness of a native, named Ippegau,
who came from a distance of thirty leagues southward to visit them. They had seen him only
once before. During one of their summer excursions, when they had lost their way, and were rowing about bewildered amongst islands unknown
to them, they accidentally encountered Ippegau.
He behaved to them in a very friendly manner,
and set them on their way homewards; and now,
in the time of their deep distress, though he knew
not of it, his heart was moved to seek them out,
and to offer to sell them regularly all the seal's
flesh he could spare. As spring advanced, this
resource failed them, and they became so feeble
for want of proper nourishment, that they could no
longer row their boat. Still they trusted in God,
and their confidence was not put to shame.

One day in May, when they had just returned
hungry and weary from an unsuccessful search
after food, word was brought them that a Dutch
ship had arrived off the coast, having on board a
cask of provisions consigned to them. This most
welcome gift came from a friend in Amsterdam, to
whom they were personally unknown. It was
accompanied by a letter from the donor, who requested that the missionaries would inform him of
their circumstances and wants; and in after years
the mission was materially assisted by the contributions of this generous benefactor and his friends.

The supplies which he had now forwarded, not only relieved them from present distress, but helped to avert similar sufferings in the succeeding winter. For the community at Herrnhut, composed as it was of poor exiles labouring for their daily bread, was able to forward but a scanty stock of necessaries to the brethren in Greenland, where, however, the mission household was about to be augmented by the arrival of Matthew Stach's widowed mother and his two sisters, the elder of whom was twenty-two, the younger only twelve years of age. They came out to take charge of the domestic concerns of the mission, and to labour in any way which might be opened to them for the good of the Greenland women and children. Matthew immediately began to teach his sisters Greenlandic, in which their progress, and especially that of Anna, the youngest, surpassed his expectations. Both eventually became wives of missionaries, and were spared to labour to old age in the service of the mission.

Towards the close of summer, Christian Stach embarked for Europe, that he might take counsel with the brethren at Herrnhut, and elsewhere, about the state and prospects of the mission. Having first visited Germany, he proceeded to England and Holland, in both of which countries resided some principal friends of the brethren. To these he communicated all that had been done, and prayed for their advice concerning the future prosecution of the work. Some useful suggestions were offered, but it was the general opinion that much must be left to the Christian discretion of the labourers, in so new and distant a field. The only rule laid down was, that when the missionaries should, at length, be so favoured as to gather souls from amongst the heathen unto Christ, their ministrations in the native congregations should be conducted, as nearly as possible, in conformity with the ritual and discipline which were observed by the United Brethren in Europe. With respect to the temporal circumstances of the mission, Count Zinzendorf and other friends lost no time in taking the necessary steps to prevent the recurrence of such seasons of privation and distress as Christian and his companions had endured the last year.

Although the present aspect of the mission was so unpromising, Christian Stach's account of it awoke lively sympathy in many hearts. In Holland a young man named Margraf, desired permission to join in the work. He was accordingly set apart for missionary service, and travelled with Stach to Copenhagen, whence they sailed for Greenland, after receiving an assurance of the king's approbation couched in very gracious terms. Margraf, however, was not able to labour long in that rigorous climate. The hard bodily as well as mental toil, which fell to the lot of each of the missionaries, joined to the extreme cold, proved too much for his strength. The first year of his residence in the country was remarkable for the unusual severity of the winter. The journal of one of the European residents records, that spirits froze like water though placed near the fire; the salted meat was hewn out of the barrels like lumps of solid ice, and when put into the pot the outside was thoroughly boiled before the inside could be pierced with a knife. In the chimney of his room the ice extended down the pipe to the very mouth of the stove, though a fire was kept burning all day, and when he rose in the morning the pillows of the bed were thickly coated with hoar frost from the congelation of his breath during the night.

Before the frost set in, the brethren had voyaged southward among a multitude of islands, where they found some natives whom they had seen before, and also their old friend Ippegau. He gave them a friendly reception, but when they endeavoured to discourse with him on religious subjects he was little inclined to listen. The other Greenlanders plainly intimated, that although they were well pleased to receive a visit from the missionaries, they did not wish them to remain long in that neighbourhood. Matthew Stach, however, anxious to improve his knowledge of the language, prevailed upon them to allow him to continue amongst them for a few weeks. He found his hosts very changeable: "Sometimes," he writes, "they listen while I read a passage of Scripture, tell me they believe all I say, and desire me to remain longer, that I may tell them more. At another time they turn angrily away, and bid me hold my peace." Worse than this, they frequently made the sacred things of which he spoke the subjects of profane ridicule and jesting. "My soul," he says, "is often in a flame when they mock my God." All the children were his friends, and would run to meet him whenever he appeared. Sometimes a little group gathered round him to listen quietly while he talked, and asked them questions, striving to insinuate into their young minds some notions of Christian truth. But these fits of attention were short-lived, as may be supposed.

Matthew returned to New Herrnhut in time to celebrate the Christmas festival with his brethren. Never had they been more keenly sensible of the contrast between the joyful remembrances and hopes which inspired their own hearts at that sacred season, and the cheerless ignorance and unbelief which pervaded the minds of the Greenlanders. Yet the missionaries were not without a lively expectation, almost a presentiment, that the long night of heathen darkness was drawing to its close. "Let us believe," they write to their friends in Germany, "that the Lord will still do glorious things in Greenland. Do not cease your supplications that God would display His power in the hearts of this poor people." It may be mentioned here that the brethren had hitherto supposed it necessary to declare to the natives in the first place, the being and attributes

of God, His righteous laws, and the punishment
which must overtake those who transgress them.
They had, indeed, laid it down as a rule, that
their chief object should be to proclaim the redemption of fallen man by the Lord Jesus Christ,
but they thought it necessary first of all to impress the minds of the Greenlanders with a sense
of accountability to an Almighty, All-just Creator,
and with a conviction that they were deeply
guilty and sinful in His sight.   Little or no effect
had, however, been produced by this mode of
instruction, and the brethren were about to be
taught by experience that there was a wiser,
more effectual way, of reaching the hearts of their
hearers.

At the beginning of June, a party of South-
landers on their way to some of the summer fish-
ing-stations, called at New Herrnhut. They were
strangers to the missionaries, and came from a
part of the country where neither the Christian
teachers, nor the things which they taught, had
yet been heard of. All the brethren, excepting
John Beck, were absent, engaged in various outdoor occupations; Beck was writing out a translation of the Four Evangelists. The strangers
watched him for a little while with surprise,
and then asked what he was doing. He explained the nature of his employment to them,
as well as he could, upon which they further requested that he would tell them what he had
written. He read a few passages to them, and

then entering into conversation with them, asked
if the spirit within them, which understood, and
thought, and hoped, and feared, would die when
the body died. All answered, "No." "But," said
John Beck, "where will the spirit be when the
body has perished?" Some said, "Up yonder,"
pointing to the sky; others, "Down beneath the
sea." For the Greenlanders entertained various
notions concerning the abode of departed spirits;
some placing it under the earth, or in the depths
of the ocean, and supposing the deep chasms in
the rocks to be the avenues which led to it; and
others fixing it on high, above the rainbow.
"And who," continued John Beck, "made the
body which dies, and the spirit which dies not,
and the earth, and sea, and sky?" They replied,
"We do not know; no one has ever told us. But
it must certainly have been some very great and
mighty one." "Truly," said John Beck, "it was
One who has all might, all wisdom, all goodness,
who created the heavens, and the earth, and all
things that are therein. He made all things good,
and last of all He created man in His own image,
to love Him and to be perfectly happy in obeying
His commandments. But man disobeyed his
Maker, and became lost in wickedness and misery.
Yet his Creator had pity on him, and the Almighty Son of God even became man that He
might redeem men from destruction, by enduring
the punishment due to their sins." The people
listened gravely and silently, and John Beck

with a glowing heart and a tongue loosed as it had never been before, told them at large how Jesus had suffered for men's salvation. Then taking up his book again, he read the account of our Lord's agony in the garden of Gethsemane. As soon as he had finished, one of the Green-

JOHN BECK TEACHING THE GREENLANDERS.

landers, named Kajarnak, stepped up to the table, and said with great earnestness, "How was that? O tell me that once more, for I would fain be saved too!" "These words," says the missionary, "the like of which I had never heard from a

Greenlander before, melted my heart, and made
my eyes overflow with joyful tears, while I related the history of the Saviour's life and death,
and strove to explain to my hearers the way of
salvation by faith in Him." His auditors were
variously affected by this discourse. Some, indeed, when their curiosity was satisfied, began to
find the subject too serious for them, and slunk
silently away, but many remained. Some laid
their hands upon their mouths, according to the
custom of the Greenlanders when struck with
surprise, and several desired that the missionary
would teach them what they should say to this
great Lord and Saviour, and repeated the prayer
they were taught, again and again, lest they
should forget it. Meanwhile the other missionaries had returned from their several employments
out of doors, and saw, with delight and astonishment, a crowd of natives listening eagerly to the
story of man's redemption. At taking leave, the
Greenlanders said, " We shall soon visit you again
to hear more of these things, and we shall tell our
neighbours what you have been saying to us."

Accordingly, a few days afterwards, some of the
party returned, and were so much interested that
they remained all night to hear more. Kajarnak,
especially, had retained a lively recollection of
the things which he had heard, and of the petitions which he had been instructed to offer to
God ; and he declared that he often felt his heart
inclined and, as it were, *bidden* to pray. All that

he heard from the missionaries he repeated to his tent companions, but took especial delight in teaching his wife and little son. After a short time he removed, and pitched his tent close to New Herrnhut, that he might be daily within reach of his instructors. "It is evident," write the missionaries at this time, "that the Word of God has made a very deep impression on the mind of this man. While we explain to him the Scriptures, words of prayer rise to his lips, and he is often moved to tears. His quick apprehension and affectionate reception of the truth are astonishing, compared with the supine indifferent temper which characterizes the natives of this country generally. Kajarnak seems to devour the words which we utter, and the truth no sooner enters his ears than it finds a lodgment in his understanding and memory." The change which had passed over their countryman aroused the curiosity and interest of several other Greenlanders, who also came and pitched their tents near the mission-house in order, as they said, to hear the joyful news of a Redeemer; and when the missionaries, addressing their native hearers, hesitated for want of suitable expressions, Kajarnak, out of the fulness of his heart, suggested appropriate words. "If we are teaching him to think," say the brethren, "he in return is teaching us to speak rightly concerning divine things."

In these new and happy occupations the summer wore on. The season of the reindeer hunt, which was prosecuted with great vigour and success in the neighbourhood of Baal's River, was now come. A number of families usually united in the chase; the women and children surrounding a district in which the reindeer were known to be plentiful, and gradually moving onwards till they closed round them, and drove the timid creatures into the narrow central space, where they were easily killed by the hunters. Another way was for the women to chase a number of reindeer into a narrow bay where the men had stationed themselves in their kayaks, ready to dispatch them with bows and arrows. The labours of the day were frequently succeeded by a feast or dance in the evening; and the hunt was in great favour among the Greenlanders, as an occasion both of profit and amusement. The missionaries were consequently more sorry than surprised, when most of the attentive listeners who had lately gathered round them took their leave to join in the chase, promising, however, to return to New Herrnhut, as soon as the hunting season was over. Kajarnak alone refused to go. He could not bear to deprive himself during some weeks of all religious instruction, and he feared that when surrounded only by his heathen fellow-countrymen, he might become indifferent to the glad tidings he had so lately learnt to prize. This was too truly the case with his companions. They returned, indeed, to the mission station towards the beginning of winter, but the religious impressions which had seemed so vivid, had faded from their minds, and after some weeks they finally left the neighbourhood.

They did their utmost to persuade Kajarnak to depart with them, representing in strong terms the difficulties he would have to encounter, and contrasting the restraints imposed on him by his new associates and pursuits, with the wild unbounded freedom of native life. Their arguments had no effect, for he had found a prize, for the sake of which he was willing to endure greater trials than any which his companions had suggested. By the desertion of his partners, Kajarnak was deprived of the large boat, tent, and other possessions in which he had an equal share with themselves, and was reduced for a time to great straits; but he bore the loss patiently. The missionaries discovered that this was the third time he had been thus impoverished, owing to his opposition to the evil practices of his comrades; and they concluded from thence, that even before he had heard of a Saviour, the Holy Spirit had been preparing his heart for the kingdom of God. Besides Kajarnak and his wife, about twenty natives settled at New Herrnhut for the winter. They were assembled daily for prayer and catechising; and on Sunday, a larger portion of time was devoted to these exercises, and to the reading and careful explanation of a portion of Scripture. By degrees, the brethren rendered into Greenlandic several portions of the Moravian liturgy. They

also translated some German hymns for the use of
their catechumens, and found that the lessons of
the Gospel expressed in verse, made a deeper impression on the minds of the natives than the same
Divine truths conveyed in the form of prose.

The number of their hearers was increased after
Christmas, by the extreme severity of the weather.
The excessive cold which marked the beginning
of the year 1738 has been already noticed; the
frost which ushered in the year 1739 was not less
severe. The surrounding seas were blocked up
with ice. Fishing and seal-hunting were entirely
suspended during several weeks. Many persons
perished of hunger; many of cold, because they
could get no seal-oil to replenish the lamps which
warmed their dwellings. Some fled to Godhaab,
entreating the Danish colonists to relieve their
distress, and from fifteen to twenty needy persons
were sheltered and fed at New Herrnhut. The
men of this company, finding their provisions
exhausted while they were still far from the
settlement, took their kayaks upon their heads,
and travelled over the ice with all the speed they
could make, to entreat succour for their wives and
children. The brethren, accompanied by a party
of boatmen from Godhaab, immediately set out
upon this charitable service; but tempestuous
weather and the ice interposed so many obstacles
to their progress, that a week elapsed before they
could reach the poor creatures, who had been
lying on the snow for the last ten days, and had

barely sustained life by eating some of the old skins which covered them.

Many times this winter, the missionaries were constrained to render hearty thanks to God for the change in their circumstances. But two years before, they had been suffering the utmost distress from hunger, accounting themselves happy if they could buy such bones and offal as even the Greenlanders were ready to throw away. Now they had not only enough for their own wants, but daily fed a company of famishing persons from their table. They prayed and endeavoured that the souls of these poor people might be nourished. Several listened attentively when the Gospel was preached to them, and when spring returned, and most of the fugitives went back to their homes, one family chose rather to fix their abode near the missionaries. All promised to settle, during the following winter, in the neighbourhood of New Herrnhut, that they might be further instructed in the things of God. As soon as the weather would permit, Kajarnak and several of the catechumens went over to Kangek, and took up their abode there for a short time, in hope to capture seals. John Beck accompanied them, to watch over his own little flock, and also to proclaim the Gospel to the numerous heathen who dwelt there, and in the neighbouring islands. The seal-hunting proved very successful, but the party from New Herrnhut were eager to bring it to a close as soon as possible. The change which had passed on

Kajarnak, and in a less degree upon others, who had not made equal progress in religious knowledge and experience, was very plainly seen, now that they were obliged daily to associate with the untaught heathen. The latter celebrated the success which crowned their labours with noisy feasts and dances, almost every night. For these revelries the catechumens had lost all taste, and when their daily work was ended, they withdrew quietly, finishing, and, if possible, beginning, every day with prayer, and a few words of exhortation from the missionary. John Beck found some opportunities of speaking with the heathen; and from this time he and his brethren frequently visited the islands.

They found that, by constant practice, they spoke and preached much more easily to themselves, and more intelligibly to the natives, who often welcomed their visits, and at times displayed considerable emotion whilst listening to their discourse, but gave no evidence, at present, that the truth had found entrance into their hearts. On the other hand, the brethren were often shocked and distressed by the barbarous actions committed amongst these people. The best and worst features of the native character were displayed in their parental and filial relations. In general, parents evinced great fondness for their children; and the children, when grown to maturity, treated their parents with gratitude and respect. But there were frightful exceptions; and various

instances of a decrepit father or mother being
buried alive, by their unnatural offspring, came to
the knowledge of the missionaries. Whenever an
opportunity of interference was afforded them,
they endeavoured to prevent the commission of
these atrocities. But Greenland was, in the
strictest sense, a land without judges, and without
laws; and the barbarous sons and daughters who
were capable of intending parricide, usually found
means to carry their wicked design into effect,
when no Europeans were near at hand. The
journals and letters of the missionaries record the
thankfulness with which they turned from these
bitter fruits of the unrenewed heart, to mark the
fear of sin, the gratitude to God, and goodwill to
their neighbours, which appeared in the little
flock under their care. Kajarnak was deeply concerned for his unbelieving countrymen, often
entreating them no longer to remain in darkness,
ignorant of their Maker, who had now sent His
word to them. Sometimes, with irrepressible
earnestness, he would pour forth a short fervent
prayer that God would enlighten them by the
knowledge of Himself. He had daily some fresh
inquiries to make concerning the things contained
in the Scriptures. One day, when speaking with
his teachers, the conversation turned upon the
conflict which every Christian has to wage with
the sin of his own heart. "When an evil
thought arises in my mind," said Kajarnak,
"wherever I am, I raise my heart silently to

Jesus, and ask Him to deliver me from it by His blood."

The missionaries were extremely slow and cautious in administering baptism to their catechumens, knowing that all eyes would be on the new converts, and that the course of the Gospel would be grievously impeded, should the subsequent conduct of the baptized be inconsistent with their Christian profession. But they could no longer delay compliance with the request of Kajarnak, that he and his family might be incorporated into the Church of the Redeemer. On Easter-day, 1739, Kajarnak and his wife, who now received the names of Samuel and Anna, made a distinct confession of their faith in Christ, before a full congregation of Europeans and Greenlanders. Having declared that they utterly renounced all heathenish customs and superstitions, and were resolved, by the help of God, to live in obedience to His commands, they were baptized, with their two little children, by Matthew Stach. The words of the baptismal formulary, " I baptize thee in the name of the Father, and of the Son, and of the Holy Ghost, into the death of Jesus," made a deep impression upon the other catechumens, who expressed an earnest desire to share the privilege which had been bestowed upon their friends. Thoughts of gratitude, and joyful hope of blessings yet to come, cheered all hearts in the little community at the mission settlement. But these pleasing anticipations were soon very sadly obscured.

It has been already observed that Greenland was a land without laws. But there was little fierceness or passion in the character of the natives, generally, and there would have been few outbreaks of violence and murder, had it not been for the blood-feuds which descended from father to son, sometimes through several generations. Occasionally a man slew his neighbour in a sudden fit of resentment, or even in deliberate malicious ill-will, but a blood-feud most commonly originated in a suspicion of witchcraft, when some man or woman was accused by the Angekoks (or sorcerers) of having caused the death of another by charms and conjurations. In any of these cases, however, the relatives of the deceased person held themselves bound to avenge his death. They usually watched for an opportunity of killing the slayer of their kinsman secretly; and would nourish their design for years, if necessary, in order to make more sure of their revenge. Nor was it only the actual murderer whose life they sought; his children, parents, kinsmen, even his neighbours, were sometimes sacrificed by the avengers of blood, and thus the tragedy was prolonged through a series of murders, persons who were entirely innocent frequently falling victims. Among the kindred of Kajarnak, who abode with him at New Herrnhut, was his wife's brother, Innungeitsok. Some years before this time, Innungeitsok had been accused by an Angekok of having conjured his son to death. The Angekok

had, however, settled at a great distance in the
north, and the accused man (who was perfectly
innocent) had ceased to take any precaution
against his malice. But the sorcerer, whose
name was Kassiak, came this summer to Kangek,
accompanied by several followers whom he had
engaged to further his evil designs. Some of
these men invited Innungeitsok, who suspected
nothing, to go fishing with them, and when out at
sea stabbed him with a harpoon. He drew it
from his body, plunged into the water and swam
to shore. But the murderers followed and overtook him, covered him with wounds, and threw
him over a cliff, at the foot of which his corpse
was found, by his sorrowing relatives, some days
afterwards. The malice of Kassiak was not
satiated by this murder. It became known that
he threatened to take the life of Okkomiak, the
brother of his victim, and also that of Kajarnak.
The Danish colonists, however, exerted themselves
to apprehend him, and he was captured with
several of his gang. Kassiak confessed that he
had committed three murders with his own hand,
and had been an accomplice in four more. But as
he was not amenable to any human tribunal, and
was entirely ignorant of the Divine law, the
Danes dismissed him again. Two of his followers,
who had formerly resided at Godhaab, and had
been instructed in the Word of God, they punished
with flogging. The apprehensions of the threatened persons were rather increased than allayed

by these proceedings, which appeared to them
more likely to irritate than to intimidate their
adversaries. Okkomiak, especially, felt himself
to be in great danger; and Kajarnak sorrowfully
came to the conclusion that he ought to reconduct
his kinsman safely back to his own people in the
south. The other members of their family were
unwilling to be left behind, and in a short time
but very few individuals remained of the little congregation on which the missionaries had looked
with so much hope and satisfaction. "Our hearts,"
say they, "were very heavy; and the mission
station, deserted by so many of its inhabitants,
appeared suddenly to have become a desert."

But ere long the solitude was enlivened by the
arrival of twenty-one boats of southerners, who
had met Kajarnak and his company on their way,
and had (they said) heard from them such wonderful things concerning God, that they desired to be
farther informed upon the subject. Towards the
close of the summer, Simek, one of the fugitives,
returned with all his household, and his arrival
was followed by that of the Greenlanders who had
been sheltered and fed during the dearth at the
beginning of the year. A numerous native congregation was thus gathered, and abode at the
mission station during the winter months. There
was a general willingness to be taught, mingled
with much levity. "At one time," say the
missionaries, "our hearers are sleepy and indifferent, when we strive to instruct them from the

Scriptures; at another, their attention is awake and lively, and they are eager to become pious all at once." The children afforded them the most satisfaction. Some of them learnt to read tolerably well in the course of the winter : they became much attached to their teachers, and when in the spring the parents quitted the mission settlement, to repair to the distant fisheries, the children carried with them the books which the missionaries had prepared and written out for their use, and which, besides easy reading lessons, contained short prayers, and rules of conduct suited to their age.

Early in the summer of 1740, Frederic Bœhnisch was married to Anna Stach. In the midst of the wedding festivities, to the joyful surprise of the mission family, their dear convert and friend, Kajarnak, made his appearance among them. He had been absent a year, and had made known to many of the Southland heathen the good tidings which he had received. At first, he said, they listened with wonder and pleasure, but when, after a while, they grew tired, and turned all to ridicule, he left them undisturbed. He had carefully endeavoured to instruct his own household, and had found in solitude access to his God and Saviour. But towards the end of his stay, an ardent longing for the instruction and society of his teachers took possession of his mind, and he was now come back, resolved never again to settle at a distance from them. It appeared, in the end, that Kajarnak's

L

words and the silent eloquence of his blameless life had produced a far greater effect than he was aware of. Between three and four hundred persons eventually forsook their homes in the South, to place themselves under the instruction of the missionaries, who attributed to the words and example of Kajarnak their first desire to be taught the way of salvation. But most of these came to New Herrnhut, after Kajarnak himself had been called to his rest.

Shortly after his return to the mission settlement, the number of hearers and catechumens was increased by persons coming from the neighbouring islands, and also from places farther north. One of the new-comers was a young woman who had repeatedly begged that she might be taken into the service of the missionaries. But they, supposing her to be actuated rather by the desire of temporal benefit than that of religious instruction, had hitherto declined to comply with her request. Now, however, she came again, saying, with tears, that she could not bear to live among her heathen companions, who hated her because she would no longer conform to their customs. She was kindly received and cared for, until the brethren could find admission for her into the household of one of the Danish colonists, where, under the instruction of Mr. Drachart, the Danish minister at Godhaab, she made satisfactory progress in Christian attainments, and at the end of a few months was baptized. Two other young women, having them-

selves laid hold of the truth, took every opportunity of recommending it to their neighbours.
One of them was endowed with considerable natural
ability, and proved a very useful assistant in the
missionary work among her countrywomen. She
was the only person amongst her own kindred and
companions whose heart was opened, at once, to
receive the Gospel. When the missionaries first
visited these people, they perceived that, while
all besides listened to their discourse with indifference or aversion, one daughter of the house had
covered her face with her hands to conceal her
tears, and heard her softly sob forth, " Oh, Lord !
Let thy light break through the very thick darkness." From that time she was wont to retire to
solitary places among the rocks to pray. One of
the brethren, who chanced to see her kneeling
half hidden behind a cliff in a lonely spot on the
shore, asked her why she knelt. "Because,"
replied she, " I now begin to believe. I pray
every day to God to be gracious unto me." Her
petitions breathed the desires of a contrite heart.
"Lord Jesus!" she was heard one day to say,
"Thou knowest that my heart is thoroughly
depraved. Make me truly sorry for it, take away
the bad thoughts, and form me according to Thy
pleasure. And as I yet know but little of Thy
Word, give me Thy Holy Spirit to instruct me."
Her constant care to avoid evil, and her value for
the instructions of the missionaries, were resented
by her relatives, who felt that her example was a

reproof to themselves, and they treated her with a degree of harshness, and even cruelty, which was of rare occurrence in a Greenland household. She escaped from them, at last, and found an asylum with Anna Kajarnak, at New Herrnhut.

The missionaries now began to prepare her for baptism. Her joy at being made acquainted with the nature and design of that holy ordinance was very great. "Now," said she, "I believe that Jesus is the friend of sinners, not because you have told me so, but because I feel it in my own heart." She received at her baptism the name of Sarah, by which she is frequently mentioned in the journals of the mission, as visiting and exhorting the heathen strangers who came into the neighbourhood. "Kajarnak and Sarah," say the brethren, "have rendered us material assistance in the translation of the 'Harmony of the Four Gospels' into Greenlandic, frequently directing us to the use of apt expressions which no grammatical knowledge would have enabled us to discover." "The testimony of our baptized Greenlanders," they add, "and especially of Kajarnak and Sarah, is producing a powerful effect upon their heathen fellow-countrymen, who cannot make the same objections to it which they have often done to ours; saying, for instance, 'You are a different sort of people from us; these things may be very good for you, but we do not need them;' or, 'We have no time to learn these things; they are too high for us; we must go a

fishing.' The heathen now see their own countrymen and equals so changed that they may well
be called new creatures, and hear them declare,
freely and gladly, the praises of the Redeemer,
who hath called them from their former darkness
into light." The migratory habits of the people
caused the news to spread far and wide. A party
who came from a considerable distance (it was
supposed from the east side, as their dialect was
not perfectly intelligible) listened with surprise
and eagerness to the Gospel narrative. With
most of them these things, new and strange as
they accounted them, served only to gratify curiosity; but there were two, an orphan brother
and sister, in whose hearts the seed took deep
root. Their change of sentiments and conduct so
offended their neighbours, that when all were
engaged in fishing at a great distance from home,
the rest of the company secretly rowed off and
abandoned them. The two young people, thus
deserted by their earthly kindred, sought and
found a new home amongst their Christian countrymen at New Herrnhut.

A party of Northlanders, also, whose curiosity
was excited by the rumours which had reached
them, pitched their tents close to New Herrnhut
for a short time. They were above all astonished
at the prayers of their converted countrymen, and
inquired whether they also could be taught to
speak such words. "O yes," was the answer;
" when you feel your great need of a Saviour, you

will not be able to help praying to Him to help you. You will be like hungry children, who naturally ask their parents for food." During the winter following his return to the mission-station, Kajarnak was particularly active in endeavouring to turn his countrymen from their evil ways. He began to visit the various winter settlements within reach, " to tell them," as he said, " something of Jesus, the Refuge of sinners." Being on a journey a short time before Christmas, several persons prayed him to remain a little while amongst them, and join in the feasts and rejoicings with which they were about to celebrate the yearly sun-feast. He replied, " I have another joy now, for a brighter sun has risen in my heart. I am hastening to my teachers to keep with them a great festival, in token that the Creator of all things was born into the world as a poor infant for our redemption."

His useful course was soon arrested by death. In February, 1741, he was attacked with pleurisy, and after a few days of acute suffering fell asleep. He uttered no complaint; and seeing his wife and kindred weeping, he said to them, " Do not be grieved for me. Have you not heard that believers when they die go to our Saviour, and partake of His joy? You know that He chose me first of our nation to know Him, and now He calls me first home to Himself. Only continue faithful to Him, and we shall all meet again before the throne of the Lamb." " All things," he said afterwards,

" which I heard in the days of my health are much clearer to me now." The excellent character of Kajarnak had won him much respect from the European settlers; and the two Danish ministers, factors, and other inhabitants of the colony joined the missionaries and his own people in attending his remains to the grave. Behind the station, at a little distance towards the north, the brethren had prepared a burial-ground as neatly as the rocky nature of the soil would permit. Here they laid the corpse of their beloved son in the faith, after one of the Danish missionaries had addressed the assembled people from the words, " I am the resurrection and the life," and told them that a believer does not *die*, but at his departure out of this world begins truly to live. " We then," say the missionaries, " kneeled down on the snow under the open sky, and gave back to our Saviour this our firstling, with fervent thanks for the grace He had conferred upon him."

The remembrance of the kinsman and friend who had thus happily departed produced a beneficial effect upon many of the survivors. His brother's wife was not of the number who profited by it; and her death, which occurred soon afterwards, was marked by a very different spirit to the humble, tranquil confidence in which Kajarnak had committed his spirit into the hands of his Redeemer. Her husband and, yet more, her children, had listened with much interest to the preaching of the Gospel; but the former could not bring himself to give up the roving life to which he had been accustomed. In one of his expeditions to the North, about a year after his wife's decease, he lost his life. His son Kuanak, a boy of ten or eleven years old, was much endeared to the missionaries by his ingenuous and affectionate disposition. He was obliged to attend his father in his journeying from place to place, but seldom missed any opportunity of visiting his teachers when they were within reach. He had a great fear of losing the things he had learned, and falling into the ways of the heathen. "I pray often to my Saviour," said the poor boy, "not to let me wander away from Him." And the prayer was answered, though he had much to suffer from the violent character of the man who undertook his guardianship after his father's death. He was able at last to return to New Herrnhut, but arrived there a cripple, owing to the ill usage he had undergone. His sister, who was a year or two older than himself, had been taken care of by the wives of the missionaries, and was one of the best pupils in their school. Several of Kajarnak's relatives now came from the south. They said that their kinsman had told them many things about one whom he called Jesuna (Jesus); things which they did not at that time understand; but since then they had frequently thought upon them, and were now come to be more fully instructed. Nor were these empty words; for not satisfied with attending the meetings of the congregation daily to hear the Scriptures explained, they often came singly to the missionaries to have their doubts and difficulties removed, and generally concluded with some such ejaculation as this: " Oh, that God would open my eyes, and purge my ears, that I might rightly understand this matter and be happy !"

The children of Ippegau, who had, six years before, been the means of preserving the brethren from starvation, joined themselves to the believers ; and also a young man named Arbalik, whose excellent capacity and warmth of heart, joined to the simplicity with which he received the Gospel, made the missionaries hope that he would be a worthy successor of Kajarnak. The event justified their anticipation. Even before his baptism, the ready zeal of Arbalik rendered him a valuable helper to his teachers. While engaged in his daily labour he related to a woman, whom he met, the history of her of Samaria, and spoke of Christ's words, " If thou knewest the gift of God, and who it is that saith to thee, Give me to drink, thou wouldst have asked of Him, and He would have given thee living water." The Holy Spirit was pleased to apply these words to the heart of the stranger, and like the woman of Samaria, but with a deeper meaning, she said, " Give me this water." A few weeks later the missionaries visited the island where she lived, and she came to them with eager desire to hear more. It seemed indeed that she could hardly be satisfied with hearing, for after listening to their discourse the whole day, she sent her son to them at night, to pray that, as soon as they had taken needful rest and refreshment, they would come to her house and tell her more. Though unable to remove from the abode of her kindred, to live in the immediate neighbourhood of the missionaries, she proved a diligent and docile learner in the school of the Gospel. Her obedience to the truth exposed her at first to persecution; but she was enabled to persevere, nevertheless, and recommended her new faith by her consistent conduct.

Matthew Stach, who had been absent on a visit to Europe, returned in the summer of 1742, bringing with him an assistant, who was to have the care of the children. He was rejoiced to find a numerous company of catechumens under the charge of his brethren. They were still exceedingly slow in admitting any to baptism. (Too slow, many of their friends in Europe thought. But some perhaps will think the long probation to which they subjected their catechumens sufficiently justified by the fact that, at the end of twenty-eight years, but two persons out of nearly a thousand baptized had relapsed into heathenism, and one of these shortly repented and returned.) The missionaries found that self-conceit was the weed which most frequently sprang up in the hearts of their people, and choked the seed of the Word. Even Sarah was at one time ensnared by this intruder. Her successful diligence among the heathen led her to entertain high thoughts of herself. Being reminded of the miserable condition in which her Lord had found her and taken pity on her, and of the sense which, at that time, she had entertained of the evil of her heart, she burst into tears, and said, "Ah! now I plainly feel that I have gradually lost the happiness I used to enjoy. Something separates me from the Saviour. I pray, and yet do not find the way to Him." But from this time she was led to watch and pray especially against this besetting sin, and in the exercise of a lowly contrite spirit her former peace of mind was restored.

At the same time with Arbalik, Matthew Stach baptized four other young people who had been for a considerable time under instruction. One of them was Issek, the sister of Sarah, whose mother, in her dying moments, had charged this daughter to follow the example of the elder sister whom they had persecuted, and join herself to the Christians. Issek accordingly, after her mother's death, repaired to New Herrnhut, and prayed to be taught concerning the things she should believe. She received at her baptism the name of Judith, and, like her sister, proved an active helper in the instruction of her countrywomen. Arbalik, some months afterwards, was married to Sarah — the first couple whom the missionaries had united in Christian matrimony.

At the beginning of the year 1743 there were symptoms of an universal awakening amongst the

Greenlanders on the shores and islands of Baal's River. Many, indeed, who for a time listened with much interest to the preaching of the Gospel, could not resolve to live near the missionaries and receive the instruction necessary to prepare them for baptism, because this would have obliged them to give up the distant hunting-places to which they were accustomed to resort. And owing to this their first ardour gave way to comparative indifference. Yet of those who removed to a distance, several came back in after years to New Herrnhut, others prosecuted their inquiries after truth in the various settlements erected by the Danes, and were there received into the Christian church. Some, too, who never joined the congregation of believers appeared by their lives to have yielded something more than a mere outward hearing and assent to the word preached by the missionaries. From this time the whole nation held foreigners in far higher esteem than before; a change which was to be attributed chiefly to the impression left upon the wandering Greenlanders. The children participated in the general desire for instruction. One of the brethren, who was out with his gun in quest of rypen, found some little girls fishing at a hole in the ice. "Pray stay," said they, "and teach us something. Cannot you leave your shooting for another day? for we were so glad when we saw you coming. We cannot come to your house to be taught, and we want you to tell us something about Jesus, the Saviour."

By the people on the neighbouring islands, the visits of the missionaries were now always welcomed. Hearing one day that a native Christian had been accidentally drowned at Kangek, one or two of the brethren immediately rowed thither, accompanied by some of their baptized Greenlanders, to assist in interring the corpse. On arriving, they found that Arbalik had already hastened to the place, and was speaking to an attentive company of listeners of faith in the Son of God, by whom life is imparted to the dead soul. " I, poor creature," he concluded, "have but little experience, but here are my teachers, who can tell you more." The missionaries accordingly addressed the people on the subject of the Redeemer's incarnation and death. All were moved, and said, " What strange thing is this? That which you say now affects us very differently from what you used to tell us about God and the two first parents. We continually said we believed it all, but we were tired of hearing it, and thought, What signifies this to us? But now we find that there is something which interests us much." On this voyage, the brethren could not but thank and praise God who had so turned the hearts of the people, that those who had formerly despised and reviled them, now came to ask pardon ; and some who had most obstinately refused to listen to them stood by the shores as their boat passed by entreating them to land. On their return the cold was intense. Their boat was covered with so thick a coat of ice that, although they were seven in number, they could scarcely row it, and the spray which dashed over congealed so suddenly that it would have sunk them had they not used unremitted exertion to bale it out.

Amongst the heathen who had witnessed the interment was an Angekok, who, when the funeral was over, declared his intention to forsake the practice of his art. He had been brought to this resolution, he said, by a startling dream. He thought that a little child came to him out of heaven, and led him first to a place of extraordinary light and beauty, where his ears were enchanted by the sound of many voices singing melodiously. From thence his infant guide conducted him to a place of darkness, where were a multitude of unhappy prisoners who could find no way of escape from their misery. "Here," said the child, "you also must dwell if you do not turn from evil;" and at these words horror took possession of his soul. But his conductor brought him forth again into the light to a company assembled at a feast, and the food which they ate made men cease from evil. All the guests sang and rejoiced, so that he too began to sing, but one awoke him, and it was a dream. The brethren were little disposed to lay much stress upon dreams; but they knew that God is sometimes pleased to speak "in a dream . . . . when deep sleep falleth upon man, then He openeth the ears of men, and sealeth their instruction, that He may withdraw man from his purpose, and hide pride from man." And several instances occurred among the natives of a soul halting between two opinions being finally determined, by a dream, to break off from evil and follow after instruction in the Gospel. Such was the effect in this case. The Angekok utterly renounced the practice of his art, in which he acknowledged that much had been mere fraud and imposture, but declared that there had also been an interference of some supernatural agency, which he now, indeed, abhorred, but was unable to describe. He received with docility the instructions of the missionaries, and after a long period of probation was baptized. His course of life afterwards was quiet and blameless, but less marked by a thirst after increasing knowledge and enjoyment of Christian truth than that of many of his fellow-converts. And it was the opinion of the missionaries that those members of their flock who had been first led to embrace the truth by impressions acting upon the imagination rather than upon the heart, rarely attained to so much maturity in the Christian character as others.

From the accounts given both by natives, and Europeans who had occasionally been present when the Angekoks were engaged (as they pretended) in intercourse with the world of spirits, it would appear that ventriloquism and various conjuring tricks were largely employed. But several of these men, who, in after years, joined the Christian church, stedfastly asserted that, besides the deceits which they had practised, and of which they were now heartily ashamed, some agency, independent of themselves, had acted upon them, and assisted them to delude their disciples. It is certain that some amongst the Angekoks proved themselves by their crimes to be the children of him who was a murderer from the beginning. Kassiak, who had caused the death of Innungeitsok, and had since then contrived the murder of several other innocent persons, had for some time past taken up his abode in Kangek. Notwithstanding his infamous character, he was looked up to with superstitious awe by many of his countrymen. But in proportion as the truth made progress, his credit and his trade declined. He had more than once threatened that the missionaries, to whom he attributed the change in his fortunes, should not live much longer to injure him. One day in May, when all the men of the mission settlement, and all their teachers, excepting Matthew Stach, were absent hunting, Kassiak came to New Herrnhut, accompanied by so many of his followers that they quite filled the dwelling of the missionaries. Matthew knew what they had threatened, but he felt no fear, and quietly pursued the occupation in which he was engaged. After sitting still for some time, Kassiak said, "We are come to hear something good." "I am glad of it," replied the missionary; and with a short prayer that God would open their hearts, he repeated a portion

of St. Paul's discourse to the men of Athens.
"Now," said he, "I need not say anything to
prove that there is a Creator, for this you all
know." To this they agreed, with the exception
of one man. "You also know that you are
wicked people." They unanimously assented.
"Now then, I come to the main point, that you
and we have a Saviour, the same great Being who
created all things in the beginning. He lived
upwards of thirty years on earth to instruct and
bless mankind, after which He was nailed to a
cross, and slain by His countrymen, who would
not believe His words. But on the third day He
rose again from the grave, and afterwards ascended
up into Heaven. The time is now approaching
when He will come again in the clouds of heaven,
and all the dead will rise and appear before Him,
as the righteous Judge, to receive sentence, every
one according to his works. But thou, poor
man!" continued Matthew, turning to the Angekok, "how wilt thou stand aghast, when all the
souls whom thou hast hurried out of the world
shall say unto Him that sits upon the throne,
'This wicked wretch murdered us just as Thou
hadst sent Thy messengers to publish to us the
way of salvation!' What answer wilt thou then
return?" Kassiak was silent and downcast. Observing that a tremor pervaded the whole company, Matthew Stach proceeded: "Hearken to
me; I will put thee in a way to escape this tre-
mendous judgment—but delay not, lest death

M

anticipate thee, for thou art old. Fall, then, at the feet of Jesus. Thou canst not see Him, yet He is everywhere. Tell Him that thou hast heard that He loves the human soul exceedingly, and rejects no one who cries to Him for grace. Pray Him to have mercy on thee, poor, miserable man, and wash out thy sins in His own blood." With seeming emotion the Angekok promised that he would do this. He remained with his company for some hours, in a thoughtful and silent mood, and gave ear to a few words spoken by Anna Kajarnak, whose brother they had murdered. Towards evening, they departed again to their place; but from this time Kassiak's enmity towards the missionaries disappeared, and he had many subsequent interviews with them. Yet he never could resolve to seek God in earnest. His life was prolonged yet many years; and he desired that his family might receive frequent visits from the Christian teachers to be instructed in the things which concerned their souls. He also repaired frequently to New Herrnhut. "Kassiak," say the missionaries, "comes often to visit us, and listens to the Word of God with a wonderfully devout mien; but his conversion, alas! goes no farther. When we pray him to set a good example to his children, for whose welfare he seems anxious, by turning with his whole heart to the Lord; he replies, ' I am never without some inclination to do it, but my will is too weak.'" In the course of time his two sons resolved to abandon the conjuring arts in which he had instructed them, and removed to the mission station, that they might profit more constantly by the teaching of the missionaries. Both of them were eventually baptized, and now, more earnestly than ever, the brethren besought Kassiak to embrace, before it was too late, the message of salvation. But he always answered, " I am too old to learn, and have been too wicked a man to be converted. Let the young people join you that they may become wiser and better. If I could change, I would join your company, because I see that you yourselves do the things which you teach, but I am too old now. I must go on in my old way."

The growing numbers of the people who came under their charge rendered their necessary dispersion during the summer months a cause of increasing solicitude to the missionaries. As far as possible, they accompanied, or frequently visited, their scattered flock ; but it was not possible to provide for all, and everywhere, the regular instruction and opportunities of public worship, which they enjoyed while dwelling together at New Herrnhut, during the winter. And much the brethren feared that the weak might be turned out of the way, and that those even who were stronger in the Christian life might fall from grace when surrounded by heathen associates, and placed in the way of many temptations to evil. This fear had even withheld them from affording to their converts one of the most essential requisites and privileges of a Christian congregation. Seven years had elapsed since the first Greenland converts had been admitted by baptism into the Church of Christ. Many of their nation had since then been added to the flock; of whom some had already finished their course on earth, while of others the missionaries were able to say, "We rejoice and thank God for the transformation of a wild, heathenish set of people into a well-ordered family of Christians. Above all, we praise Him for the gifts of His grace manifest in the conduct of some of our baptized Greenlanders." Yet not one of these converts had hitherto been admitted by them to the Lord's Supper! At length, however, the enduring character of the good work which had been wrought, was become too evident to allow the missionaries longer to deprive their Greenland brethren and sisters of so great a blessing. Perhaps, too, we may say their own faith in the grace and faithfulness of God was stronger, so that they could more unreservedly trust in Him to sustain the spiritual life which He had imparted. They began, therefore, carefully to prepare their more advanced converts for admission to the Holy Communion. The gratitude and joy of the native communicants were affecting. "O, how is it possible," said they, "that our Saviour can love poor men so exceedingly!"

From this time, the festivals of the Church were

invested with new interest. The special services, by which the great events of the Gospel history were commemorated, proved the means of much edification to the Greenlanders. During the season of Lent, the humiliation, sufferings, and death of our Lord, formed the constant subjects of reading and illustration, but especially in Passion Week, when the missionaries strove to lead their people, step by step, through the last solemn scenes of their Redeemer's life on earth. On Easter Eve, they were reminded that by His abode in the tomb the Son of God had sanctified the grave, and made this last house (otherwise so gloomy and frightful) a place of blessed rest for those who die in the Lord. On Easter Sunday, the congregation assembled in the chapel before sunrise, and proceeding from thence to the burial-ground, they called to mind, by name, the brethren and sisters departed during the preceding year; and, in the words of their burial-service, prayed for " everlasting fellowship with them and the church triumphant around the throne of the Lamb."

Hymns, chants, and anthems, which constitute a large portion of the public services of the Moravians, became a source of great delight to the Greenlanders. Almost every evening during the winter, several of the people assembled to repeat and practise, and those who could not read, learnt the words from the lips of their better-instructed companions. Some of the brethren

who, from time to time, came out from Germany
to assist in the affairs of the mission, could play

SINGING SCHOOL.

on the flute, violin, or other instruments. Finding that several of the native youths had a good
ear for music, and were capable of learning to
play well enough to accompany the singing of the
congregation, they formed amongst them a little
band. The singing was remarkably pleasing;
the women and children possessing, in general,
sweet voices, which melted into perfect harmony.
In the morning, at eight o'clock, and also in the
evening, when the men had returned from the

sea, service was held daily in the chapel, and at one or other of these times one of the missionaries explained a passage of Scripture, or delivered a short exhortation. On Sundays, a sermon was preached in the afternoon, and many of the neighbouring heathen frequently joined the congregation. A short, special service was held on Sunday, for the benefit of the children, who were too young to participate in the more protracted devotions of their elders, and they were daily assembled to be catechized.

Before Whitsuntide, the congregation broke up for the summer, to repair to the fisheries. One or more of the missionaries usually accompanied them, and a few brief extracts from their journals will describe the kind of life led by the teachers and their people at these times. " On the 19th May," says John Beck, " I set off for the Caplin Fishery with most of our people, in twenty-two large boats and a great number of kayaks. In two hours it began to snow so thickly that not one of us could see twenty paces before him, but the good angels guided us, and no one suffered harm or was separated from his company. We were able also to pitch our tents sufficiently near together, so that until the sealing party left us none were prevented by distance from joining in our daily worship. We all had an opportunity of learning by experience that the presence of the Lord is not confined to place ; and I endeavoured to impress upon the minds of the people the assurance that the grace of our Saviour is to be sought and found not only in the house of prayer, and in the solemnities of worship, but everywhere. At sea, or on the icy mountains, or in the thickets, wherever a soul, sensible of its need, applies to Him for relief, there is the ear of the Lord open, and His arm stretched forth.

During the sermon on Whitsunday, we had a numerous and attentive auditory, though the snow fell in great quantities upon us; for the church at Pisiksarbik has no roof but the firmament, its walls are the snow-white mountains, the pulpit is a large stone, and a ledge of·rock the substitute for benches. After the service, I gave the Greenlanders a dinner of reindeer's flesh. Two of them, who had been guilty of some misconduct recently, now appeared ashamed, but one was very shy of me, and I knew he had been associating with bad companions. I sought an opportunity of conversing with him, and represented how grievous and dishonouring such conduct was to his heavenly Master. This appeared to move him much; he wept, and I could not refrain from weeping with him."

On the 28th, the tattarets* gave notice that the fish were approaching, and the first shoals of caplins came near the shore. All hands were soon busily engaged in catching them. " On the

---

* The tattaret, a beautiful little bird with sky-blue plumage, is a species of gull, which spends the winter in warmer countries, returning to Greenland early in the spring. It follows the shoals of caplins into the fiords.

8th of June, a great many heathen came to us, and heard a sermon on John iii. 17—21. The same evening our sealing party came back with the melancholy intelligence that one of their number, young Bartholomew, was missing. I despatched several men immediately to search for him. After much labour they found the poor youth in a bog, quite dead. He had tried to carry his kayak across it, seemingly, but the treacherous soil giving way beneath his feet, he had sunk in and was suffocated. He came to us last year and was baptized, and we had derived much satisfaction from his good conduct. We laid him in a grave, and raised some stones for a monument on a rock near the spot. Four days afterwards, our fishery being prosperously completed, with songs of praise we set out in fair weather for New Herrnhut."

The last night of the year was a season marked by special prayer and thanksgiving, in which were remembered the remarkable occurrences of the past twelve months; and few, if any, years passed in which some of the native Christians, and the brethren themselves, had not to give thanks for preservation in circumstances of great peril, or to own with submission the chastening hand which had removed from them one and another of their kindred and friends. Many instances of dangers and escapes at sea, when overtaken by sudden fogs, or inclosed amidst the floating ice fields, are recorded in the journals of the mission; and also some perils of a less ordinary kind, of which the following may serve as an example. In the month of May, 1745, while everything was still frozen, and the ground covered with snow, the brethren were startled one morning by a loud noise like the roar of a tempest. They had scarcely time to run out of the house before it was filled with water, which, for a moment, they supposed must proceed from a sudden thaw, melting the snow and causing the brook which watered the valley to overflow. But the frost was as hard as ever, and all around, without, continued solid as marble. In about an hour the water subsided, and they were able to re-enter their house. They then found that both there and in the storehouse the water had gushed out of the earth like a fountain. But they were never able to account for so strange a circumstance.

The year 1747 was happily distinguished by the erection of a new and larger church. The brethren had already enlarged their former place of meeting as far as possible, and for some time past had been obliged, for want of room, to preach and baptize in the open air, or if the weather was extremely cold, to separate with their flock into two or three little congregations, assembling in different apartments. This uncomfortable state of things was remedied by the liberality of their friends in Holland, who sent out timber framed ready for erecting a building seventy feet long and thirty broad. It contained, besides the church, some rooms for the missionaries; and two wings on the north and south sides comprised school-rooms and storehouses. While the erection was in progress, Matthew Stach proceeded to Europe. The brethren there thought it advisable that the missionaries stationed in Greenland should, from time to time, revisit their native climate, to recruit their strength, and rest awhile from the various labours incident to their situation. Accordingly, each of the Greenland missionaries had in turn paid a short visit to Germany. Matthew Stach was now repairing thither for the second time. He had been requested to bring with him some of the Christian Greenlanders, who had expressed a strong desire to see " the European land," and the friends who had cared for their souls, and sent teachers to show them the way of salvation.

In compliance with this request, the missionary was accompanied by Arbalik and his wife Sarah, her sister, Judith Issek, Matthew, the son of Kajarnak, a boy of fourteen, and another youth about the same age. The journey proved of great advantage to them. Their minds were enlarged by the introduction to civilized nations, to new modes of living, new forms of animal and vege-table life, while the simplicity of their religious feelings remained unimpaired. But two of the travellers did not live to return to their native land, and the journeyings of the others lasted much longer, and extended over a much larger portion of the world, than either they or their

European friends had foreseen. They arrived in
Europe towards the end of summer, and spent
the autumn and winter in Holland and North
Germany. Fearing that a longer continuance
in a climate so unlike their own, and the de-
privation of Greenland diet, might injure their
health, the missionary proposed to return with
them before the heats of summer commenced.
Various obstacles, however, arose and prevented
him from carrying this design into effect. In the
meantime Sarah peacefully ended her life at
Herrnhut, in May, and her husband Arbalik
followed her, not many weeks afterwards, to
the great grief of their teachers, who lost in
them two very valuable assistants. Matthew
Stach was now, more than ever, anxious to take
the survivors safely back to their own country;
but no opportunity of doing so was afforded him
until, towards the close of the year, the master
of the ship Irene, just arrived at Amsterdam
from New York, expressed his willingness to
reconduct the whole party to Greenland. It
was, however, by a most circuitous route, the
ship being bound to London and Philadelphia
before she could perform the Arctic voyage.
They arrived in London in the beginning of
1749. George II. being told that some Christian
Greenlanders were in England, expressed a wish
to see them, and they were accordingly presented
to the king and the rest of the royal family at
Leicester House. After remaining in port a short

time, the Irene sailed again for Philadelphia,
where the captain purposed remaining some
weeks. During this time Matthew Stach and
his companions visited the settlements formed
by some of the Moravian brethren in Pennsylvania, and their missions amongst the American
Indians in the backwoods. Much kind feeling
and brotherly sympathy was elicited by the intercourse which took place between the American
converts and their Greenland brethren. With
the help of the missionaries to interpret between
them, they interchanged accounts of the progress
of the Gospel amongst their respective nations,
and of their very different modes of life and
occupation. The Indian first converted by the
brethren was a Mohican, named Tschoope, a
man who had been notorious for his evil and
ferocious life, but who possessed much influence
over his companions. The account he gave of
his conversion deserves to be recorded. Having
been frequently amongst the Dutch settlers, he
understood their language, which induced the
Moravian missionary, Christian Rauch, who could
speak Dutch, to address himself to him in the
first place. The effect produced by his discourse
is best described in Tschoope's own words, when
addressing the other missionaries who had come
to visit him. "Brethren," said he, "I have been
a heathen, and have grown old amongst them,
therefore I know how the heathen think. Once,
a preacher came and began to explain to us that

there was a God. We answered, 'Dost thou think us so ignorant as not to know that? Return to the place from whence thou camest.' Then another preacher came, and said, 'You must not steal, nor lie, nor get drunk,' &c. We answered, 'Thou fool, dost thou think us ignorant of this? First teach the people, to whom thou belongest, to leave off these things. For who steal, lie, or are more drunken than thine own people?' And thus we dismissed him. After some time brother Rauch came to my hut, sat down, and spoke nearly as follows: 'I am come to you in the name of the Lord of heaven and earth. He sends to let you know that He will make you happy, and deliver you from the misery in which you lie at present. For this end He became a man, gave his life a ransom, and shed His blood for sinners.' Something more he said concerning the preciousness of the blood which redeemed us; then, being tired with his journey, he lay down, and slept soundly. I thought, what kind of man is this? There he lies and sleeps; I might kill him, and throw him into the wood, and who would regard it? But this gives him no concern. However, I could not forget his words. They constantly recurred to my mind. Even when asleep, I dreamt of the blood Jesus Christ shed for us. I found this to be entirely different from anything I had heard before, and I interpreted Rauch's words to the other Indians. Thus, through the grace of God, an awakening began among us.

I say, therefore, brethren, speak of Christ our Saviour, of his sufferings and death, if you would wish your words to gain entrance among the heathen."

Letters, speaking the Christian friendly feeling of the writers, were sent by these Indian converts to their Greenland brethren; and the congregation at Bethlehem, hearing that they were often reduced to straits for want of timber, sent them also a quantity of wood and shingles, sufficient to build storehouses in which all the dried fish, reindeer's flesh, &c., gathered by the labour of the summer, could be safely laid up for winter consumption. With this homely but valuable present, Matthew Stach and his companions took their leave, the Irene being now ready to depart. They arrived in Greenland late in the summer of 1749, and were joyfully welcomed back to New Herrnhut. The Greenlanders were never tired of interrogating their travelled brethren concerning all that they had heard and seen in strange countries. The travellers had so well conformed to European dress and customs, that, during the latter portion of their journeyings, no one, until told who they were, suspected them to be natives of a heathen and uncivilized land. They now resumed without repugnance the laborious life of Greenlanders, with all its inevitable hardships; but retained through the rest of their days the superior esteem of their countrymen, as persons wiser than their brethren.

Judith was very desirous to promote among her

young countrywomen the order and decorum
which characterized the Moravian sisters in
Europe. Nor were the young people or their
elders averse to co-operate in her plans. Accordingly, she erected with their help a dwelling large enough to furnish accommodation for
the unmarried young women of the settlement,
and took them to live with her. By day each
fulfilled her duties in the household to which
she belonged, but returned in the evening to
her companions. Judith was directed and assisted in her charge by the wives of the missionaries, and though young herself, proved a
kind and vigilant superintendent. She continued to labour for the temporal and spiritual
welfare of her countrywomen for ten years, after
which a lingering illness brought her to the grave.
Ever since their return to Greenland, the natives
who had been in Europe had kept up a corre-
spondence with their friends there. Some of their
letters were preserved and inserted afterwards in
the history of the mission. One, written by Judith
in the very near prospect of death, breathes a
spirit of patient submission, of humble assured
faith, and joyful anticipation of life everlasting
in the presence and service of her Redeemer,
which may be well described in the words of
the Prophet, "Thou wilt keep him in perfect
peace whose mind is stayed on Thee, because he
trusteth in Thee."

The missionaries found much to encourage them

in their schools. School was kept only during the winter; and but for half the day. For the girls were early inured by their mothers to the various labours which fell to the lot of a Greenland woman, and the boys, while still very young, began to practise rowing the kayak, darting the harpoon, &c. Much time was necessary to acquire proficiency in these exercises. Amongst the heathen Greenlanders, dexterity in their arduous occupations was reckoned the highest virtue, and nothing would have been more apt to deter them from giving ear to the Gospel, than an appearance of inactivity, negligence, or unskilfulness, in those of their countrymen who had embraced it. But short as was the portion of each day devoted to school, the children, in general, made good progress. Many learnt to read well in the course of one winter; and amongst the elder scholars, there were several who read and wrote both Greenlandic and German correctly. They were sedulously taught to regard their superior attainments as the means of benefiting others who had not enjoyed the same advantages; and their teachers were pleased to see that they often employed their leisure hours in reading to the old people who had never learned.

As a nation, the Greenlanders were, by nature, careless and improvident. The missionaries, therefore, constantly bent their efforts to form habits of economy and forethought in their people. "To mind diligently their own busi-

ness and labour, that they might walk honestly
toward all men, and might lack nothing. To
labour, that they might have to give to him that
needed. To waste nothing." These lessons were
not only inculcated by the lips of the teachers,
but taught by all the regulations which they introduced among the inhabitants of the mission
settlement, and to which the latter willingly
consented. For, it may be said here, even had
the missionaries desired to impose any rules by
constraint, the attempt would have been hateful
to the Greenlanders, who were jealous of their
liberty. But with their entire consent, such
orderly methods of industry and prudent fru-
gality were established among the Christian natives, that besides maintaining a number of helpless orphans, aged, and destitute persons, whom
their heathen kindred had rejected, they had
always a larger quantity of produce to dispose
of to the Danish factors than the latter could
procure elsewhere. " Indeed," says the old historian of the mission, " if any temporal advantage
must be confessed to have an influence in inducing
heathen Greenlanders to join the believers, it is
the prevalence of honesty and good order in our
congregation, where every one is sure of his
property, friendless widows are relieved, none
are obliged to marry against their inclination,
no wife is turned away, or husband permitted
to marry more than one wife, and all fatherless
children are maintained and educated."

Cheered by the increase with which God had blessed the seed sown by himself and his brethren, Matthew Stach began to look with a longing eye towards the south-west. There, beyond the spreading waters, an Esquimaux people, akin in race and language to his Greenland converts, wandered over the cold barren wastes of Labrador. To introduce the Gospel amongst them became now the desire of his heart. The account which the mariners, who had visited the coast of Labrador, gave of its inhabitants, was not of a character to invite men who were impelled by other motives than those of love to God and man. " Thieves and murderers," were the terms in which almost every one who spoke of these people, described their character. " But the more depraved they are by nature," said the missionary, " the more need is there that we should make known to them the way of salvation." His brethren in Europe cordially entered into his views, and authorized him to proceed to England, in order to solicit permission from the Hudson's Bay Company to begin a mission in Labrador by preaching the Gospel to the natives belonging to their factories. His application, however, though seconded by persons of wealth and influence in London, proved unsuccessful. Some pious merchants who shared in the wish of the missionary to make known the Word of God in that country now devised another plan. They agreed to fit out a ship for trading on the coast of Labrador. Missionaries, it was thought, might, by this means, visit the people and form an acquaintance with some of them, and, in the end, a mission station might be established. While Matthew Stach was waiting in England for this project to be carried into effect, the Moravian brethren in Germany deputed one of their bishops, Johannes de Watteville, to visit the Greenland congregation. De Watteville, who had just returned from visiting and inspecting the missions in North America and the West Indies, willingly undertook this new commission, but desired for his companion Matthew Stach; and the latter, foreseeing that some time must elapse before anything could be done in Labrador, gladly returned meanwhile to his flock in Greenland.

The voyage occupied six weeks. After having been hemmed in by ice-fields during many days, they discerned, on the 12th June, the snow-clad tops of the Greenland mountains, being then about twenty leagues distant from the shore. Presently afterwards, the voyagers were gratified by the appearance of one of the phenomena of polar skies, three parhelia, or mock suns, encircled by six luminous halos. "The following day," says Bishop Watteville, "we entered Baal's River, and were met near the outermost island by two of our Greenlanders, but the wind being too high for them to get on board, they kept before us swimming through the waves on their kayaks like waterfowl, and with such velocity as to be always ahead of the ship, though they were often half buried under water. The wind rapidly increased to a hard gale, and we flew past island after island like an arrow. At length New Herrnhut came in sight, moving my heart with joy and gratitude. It stood like a garden of the Lord amidst the wilderness. All around were bare rocks thinly interspersed with sand, but the land adjacent to the church and dwelling of the missionaries was clad with verdure most refreshing and grateful to the eye. In front of the church, the brethren had laid out a garden, in which they pleased themselves with raising such salads and other vegetables as could be reared in a climate where the ground was frozen during nine months in the year. On either side were the huts of the Greenlanders, built on the rocks ascending from the shore. Scurvy-grass, mountain sorrel, and other indigenous plants, grew in the greatest abundance round the buildings; and the plain between the little village and the beach was carpeted with grass, and dotted over with the summer tents of the people. A large magazine, standing alone on a height, served as a beacon to ships approaching the shore.

The bishop soon made himself acquainted with all the inhabitants of the settlement, visiting the various stations to which they had dispersed for fishing; and with the help of one of the missionaries to interpret, instructing them all both publicly and privately, he entirely won the esteem of the Greenlanders. They were accus-

tomed to distinguish persons by some epithet
descriptive of their bodily or mental qualities,
and he was long remembered among them as
Johannes *Assersok*, i. e., *the loving*. He joined his
missionary brethren in all their labours; and
records, with pleasure, some of the expeditions
in which he accompanied them to collect drift-
wood, and turf, or the eggs of the eider-fowl,
which formed an important part of their sustenance during the summer months. One of
these voyages was to Kanneisut, about ten miles
distant on the other side of Baal's River; a tract
of land broken with high rocky hills, interspersed
with thickets and plots of grass, and watered by
many streams and pools of clear water. This was
a great resort of reindeer; but it was yet more
valuable for the abundance of trout which might
be caught in the brooks, several hundred being
sometimes taken at one haul of the net. The
banks of the water, however, and the thickets,
were infested with swarms of mosquitoes. They
were not, the bishop assured his companions,
nearly so tormenting as those which abounded
on the banks of the Delaware, or in the island of
St. Thomas, whence he had lately come. The
interest and sympathy of the native Christians
were strongly excited by Bishop Watteville's account of the American brethren, who had shown
them so much goodwill a few years before; and
by his recital of the sufferings and difficulties
which harassed the converted negro-slaves of St.

Thomas. " How happy we are," exclaimed they, " in being free to serve God every day in peace !"

One of the subjects concerning which the brethren most desired to take counsel with the bishop, was the establishment of a mission-station in South Greenland, the most populous part of the country, and that from which most of their converts had originally come. These people were ardently desirous that the Gospel should be preached in their native district, and the missionaries longed to lay the foundation of another Christian settlement in the midst of the heathen. There appeared at present no prospect of their being able to do this, the means of the Moravian brethren being already tasked to the utmost to maintain the numerous missions they had planted during the last twenty years. Bishop Watteville could only join his hopes and prayers to their own, in regard to this more distant sphere of labour, but he visited with them various heathen settlements within reach of New Herrnhut. By his advice, the missionaries began to prepare some of their converts for more extensive usefulness, committing to them the duty of instructing their fellow-believers in the Word of God, during the absence of the people at their hunting and fishing-places. Matthew Kajarnak, Johanan, his friend and fellow-traveller in the visit to Europe, and several older brethren, whose exemplary conduct and progress in religious knowledge entitled them to confidence, were

formed into a company of "National Assistants."
Each had a certain number of families placed
more particularly under his charge, to watch
over them and catechise the children. In the
absence of the missionaries, the National Assistants presided over the daily assemblies for
worship, led the prayers of the people, and
read and explained the Scriptures. They were
also called upon to preach from time to time,
in the mission-church. For all these duties
they were carefully instructed by the missionaries, to whom they rendered account of their
proceedings every week. They were encouraged
also to publish the Gospel to the heathen wherever they found opportunity. One or two speci-
mens of their discourses may be quoted here.
Having spoken to a company of heathens of
the Son of God who had died for fallen man,
the teacher continued very earnestly, "So dead
and stupid as you now are, I, too, was formerly;
but when I heard that there was a Saviour who
has purchased life for poor miserable men, I
rejoiced at the good news, and prayed to Him
to give me open ears and an open heart to hear
and understand. And now you may easily see
that I am happy, and I can wish you nothing
better than that you also may submit to be made
happy." Another assistant said, " It is with
us, as when a thick mist covers the land, which
hinders us from seeing and knowing any object
distinctly. But when the fog disperses, we get

sight of one corner of the land after another; and when the sun breaks forth, we see everything clear and bright. Thus it is with our hearts. While we remain at a distance from our Saviour, we are dark, and ignorant of ourselves; but the nearer approaches we make to Him the more light we obtain in our hearts, and thus we rightly learn to discover all good in Him and all evil in ourselves."

That not only the foreigners—whom they regarded as different people from themselves—but their own countrymen, should speak of an invisible, almighty Saviour, Intercessor, and Friend, with the tone of men who *knew* Him in whom they believed, made a powerful impression upon many. "Hast thou seen the God of whom thou speakest?" said a heathen man to one of the brethren. He replied, "I have not seen Him yet, but I love Him with my whole heart, and I and all true believers shall one day see Him with our bodily eyes." The inquirer went away thoughtfully, and pondered the answer he had received. Afterwards he came to New Herrnhut, and prayed to be admitted into the number of catechumens. After receiving suitable instruction, he was baptized, and led a life consistent with his Christian profession. The cheerfulness of his piety was remarkable, and his example was the more valuable, because he was the head of a numerous family, and a man much esteemed among his countrymen for sense and uprightness.

Within a short time after the appointment of the National Assistants, a fatal sickness broke out in the neighbourhood of the settlement. Thirty of the native Christians, amongst whom were some of the brethren so recently selected to serve as helpers, died, and also many of the heathen dwelling on the islands. Above all, the missionaries were grieved at the loss of Matthew Kajarnak, beloved for his father's sake and his own. "His activity and sound judgment," they write, "made him a very valuable fellow-labourer. We rejoice indeed with him that he is at rest, but his name will never be mentioned among us without exciting a feeling of affectionate regret." His end, like his father's, was full of peace, though attended with much bodily suffering. The breaches which death had made in the congregation were much more than filled up in the succeeding twelve months. Amongst those who now joined themselves to the believers, was a man named Kainaek, a wealthy Southlander, of a family esteemed noble in Greenland, since during three generations the men had been renowned seal-catchers. But Kainaek was even more conspicuous for his unbridled violence of character, than for his skill and wealth. He had been long acquainted with the missionaries, but his feelings towards them in former years had been anything but friendly. A young woman whom he sought in marriage was so terrified by his furious temper, that she fled from her own friends to the mission settlement, entreating the white people to protect her. The missionaries pitied her distress, and gave her an asylum, which so incensed Kainaek, that he attempted to take the lives of some of the native Christians. In this evil design he was frustrated; but he found an opportunity, after some time had elapsed, of carrying off his intended bride. His union with her proved the means of his conversion. During her abode at New Herrnhut she had heard something of the Word of God. She desired to hear more, and she acquired sufficient influence over Kainaek to make him a frequent listener to the discourses of the missionaries. But it was long before he could bring himself to embrace the humbling doctrine which they preached. Restless and unhappy, he wandered from south to north, and from north to south again, but could not fly from himself. At last, one terrible winter's day, the inhabitants of New Herrnhut were rejoiced by the arrival of Kainaek and his whole family. The travellers were covered with ice as with a coat of mail, but the fire was kindled within, and they had come with humble minds, earnestly desiring to be taught and baptized into the obedience of Christ.

Kainaek became as remarkable after his baptism for his quiet humble course of life, as he had been formerly for unrestrained vehemence. He had occupied so conspicuous a place among his countrymen, that his conversion awakened attention and curiosity in many who had as yet heard little or nothing of the Gospel. And now, for some months, there were few weeks or even days in which strangers did not visit New Herrnhut, to inquire what these new things were? The interest with which some of the new-comers listened to the Word of God excited lively joy and hope in the breasts of their Christian countrymen. One of the national assistants, Daniel Agusina, became inspired with an ardent desire to visit his kindred and former acquaintances, who were living three hundred miles to the northward, that he might declare to them the things he had learned.

The missionaries feared the temptations to which he would be exposed when surrounded by the heathen, and deprived of public worship and pastoral instruction. But seeing that his heart was set upon going they gave their consent and provided him with a companion, one of his fellow-assistants, named Jonas, who also had kindred in the north. The two travellers set out, full of hope, and turned their voyage into a missionary excursion, by making known the tidings of a Redeemer wherever they could find hearers. In some places they were much ridiculed and reviled; in others, they met with attentive listeners; and at the end of two months they returned with grateful hearts, accompanied by several of their kindred. Daniel had persuaded all the surviving members of his family to come with him to New Herrnhut, and eventually all were converted to the faith. He possessed no ordinary qualifications as a teacher; and of all the national assistants he appears to have been the one who possessed most influence, and whose labours were the most blessed. By birth he was a Southlander, the son of a rich and prudent man, who led, according to the custom of the country, a roving life, residing one year in the south, another at Kangek, a third at Disko, &c. Agusina was the oldest of a numerous family, and was born about the time that Egede, the father of Greenland missions, landed in the country; but he had grown to manhood before the tidings of a Saviour reached his ears. His father being at that time in Kangek, was visited by Mr. Drachart, the Danish minister at God-haab, who preached the Gospel to him and his family. Agusina was so impressed by what he heard that day, that he determined at once to become the property of the Saviour who had redeemed him. But he could not at this time join himself to the believers, as he desired to do. His father required his services, and Agusina was obliged to accompany him through a long course of wanderings. At length the family came again to Kangek, and Agusina, who was now a married man, with children of his own, claimed his right to act independently. His brothers had grown up, and were able to take his place in assisting their father; he now, therefore, bade adieu to his kindred, and removed to Godhaab to place himself under the instruction of M. Drachart, by whom, in the year 1747, he was admitted into the Church, receiving at his baptism the name of Daniel. But one of his uncles having settled at New Herrnhut, and become a Christian, Daniel became very desirous to join him, and with the willing consent of Mr. Drachart, and the permission of the Moravian missionaries, he placed himself under the pastoral care of the latter. He was soon afterwards admitted to the Holy Communion, and from that time became ardently desirous to publish to his countrymen the good news which he had himself received. Having been received into the company of assistants about the year 1753, he gave himself with all his might to the work. "Out of the abundance of his heart, his mouth overflowed, early and late," write the missionaries. Sometimes his heathen countrymen received his words with mockery, but more often they manifested a particular esteem for him, and veneration for his words. For he showed discretion as well as zeal in his efforts to instruct them. When addressing men who had never heard the Word of God, he would enter into friendly discourse with them, interest himself in their affairs, and by degrees, giving a different turn to the conversation, would draw forth the thoughts they had concerning a Creator, and a future state. In this manner he often led them to acknowledge that man was by nature prone to evil, and could not find favour in the eyes of a perfectly pure and righteous Lord. Then with a burning heart, and often with tears in his eyes, he used to speak to them of Jesus. "What happiness it was," said he, looking back on his death-bed to these seasons,—"what joy it was to lead my countrymen to the Saviour, and to see them as happy as He, through mercy, has made me!" He was much respected by the Danish colonists and factors, who commonly spoke of him as "the man of God." Sometimes, during the busy season of the trade and fisheries, Daniel was obliged by necessary business to remain for a day or two at some station, where, excepting the factor and his boat's crew, all around him were heathens. At these times, the Greenlanders generally asked him to discourse to them, when their day's work was over, and he never refused. "But," said the factors, relating these things afterwards to the missionaries, "without any hesitation because of the presence of Europeans, Daniel used to uncover his head, fold his hands reverently together, and, after first praying, would speak to the heathen in so earnest and affecting a manner, that they were often moved to tears, and used to remain together conversing about what they had heard till a late hour of the night. Daniel spoke much in similitudes, knowing that this mode of teaching

was most acceptable to his countrymen. In
winter, when he had much leisure, he would place
himself in his kayak, and go to visit heathen
villages inaccessible to the boat of the missionaries.
Of a lively intrepid spirit, he was not to be
deterred by danger, especially if he knew that
any soul had been awakened to desire instruction.

In all these labours he appeared to be guided by
a spirit of unaffected humility. "In all places,"
said he one day to the missionaries, "I pray to
the Saviour to lead and direct me; for I know that
I am a poor and wretched man if He is not continually near me. My faults and infirmities are
numberless, but my Lord knows them all, for He
knows my heart, and therefore, I at all times address
Him as a sinner. But the Holy Spirit directs my
heart to the sufferings of Jesus, and I feel that He
loves me who always chooses the poorest of men."
But after persevering in his course of humble zealous diligence for several years, Daniel said, perhaps, in his heart, "I shall never be moved," and
too soon had occasion to say "My feet were almost
gone, my footsteps had wellnigh slipped." "By
a trivial circumstance," write the missionaries,
"the door was opened for self-complacency at the
great and excellent gifts which Daniel really
possessed, though he had always appeared un-
conscious of them; and we could not but perceive
that his love for Christ and souls had lost something of its former earnestness and simplicity,
and that his discourses no longer went home, as

heretofore, to the hearts of the hearers." The Master, whom, notwithstanding all infirmities and defects, he sincerely served, did not permit him to continue in this state of spiritual declension. He brought him back by trial. His only daughter, Beata, a very dutiful and promising child of fifteen, died after a few days' illness, to the extreme grief of her father, whose dearly beloved companion and helper she had been. His distress in mind was at first so great, that he withdrew from participation in those ordinances of divine worship which had been his greatest joy. But after a few weeks the agitation of his spirit was calmed. He recognized the justice and mercy of God's dealings with him, humbled himself beneath the chastening hand of his Heavenly Father, and found peace. "For His anger endureth but a moment; in His favour is life."

Very soon afterwards, Daniel was seized with mortal sickness. But the prospect of death no more distressed him; and when the disease left his mind clear, almost all his words were of grateful praise. "That my Lord hath chosen me from among the heathen—that He has washed me from my sins—that he has given me His body to eat, and His blood to drink; and has kept me in fellowship with Himself, even until now—oh, how will I thank and praise Him!"

In bringing to a close the history of Daniel Agusina, we have passed over a period of nine or ten years, during which the work of the missionaries continued on the whole to prosper, though not without many disappointments—some of which arose from the death of native converts who had proved themselves faithful brothers and sisters in Christ, and some from the speedy effacing of religious impressions in hearts which had appeared to be touched by Divine grace. " I know not how it is," said a woman : " we always *will be* converted, yet nothing comes of it ; we still prefer other things before our Saviour." Like the men who refused to come to the marriage feast, the Greenlanders had many excuses for declining to give heed to the Gospel. " I would gladly come to this Saviour," said one young man, " but my relations always keep me back." Another had bought a great deal of powder and shot, " which," said he, " I must first use up in the South, where there are many reindeer." Some men who would fain have settled within reach of the missionaries, were hindered by their wives, who could not bear to give up the feasts and merry-makings they had been used to share with their neighbours. One of these women came afterwards in great sorrow to the brethren. Her husband, she said, had lately died, praying earnestly for the pardon of his sins, and had entreated, as a last favour, that his corpse might be carried to New Herrnhut, and buried near the Christians, with whom he had desired to live. She bitterly lamented now that she had opposed his wishes, and prayed that the missionaries would take her into the number of their

catechumens. In general, the young people received the word with most readiness, and were
often the means of drawing their parents to join
the believers. A man, to whom the brethren had
often spoken in their missionary excursions, but
who could not resolve to leave his native place to
obtain more full and regular Christian instruction,
accidentally met his daughter at the caplin fishery.
She had removed from home some time before,
and had become a Christian. He angrily reproached her with separating herself from her
father and kindred, and taking up with new
friends; but she met his reproaches by modestly
stating the reasons which had induced her to take
this step; and having spoken of the peace which
was obtained by obeying the Word of God, she
said, "You too, my father, may share in this happiness; but if you will not, I cannot stay and
perish with you." These simple words appeased
his wrath, and softened his heart. And not long
afterwards he repaired to New Herrnhut, bringing with him his two sons, and the rest of his
family. "I wish that my children may be baptized," he said to the missionaries, "for they are
young, and they desire to belong to Jesus. As
for myself, I dare not think of such a favour,
being very bad, and old too. Yet I will live and
die amongst you, for it refreshes my heart to hear
of the Saviour."

But there were also several cases in which the
parents could not be persuaded, and either en

deavoured by force to carry away their children from the mission settlement, or angrily renounced all further intercourse with them.

Some of the years now under review were distinguished by seasons of excessive cold and scarcity. In 1757, all navigation being stopped for some months by the ice, a famine prevailed, accompanied by the usual shocking consequences among the heathen, of old, helpless persons being buried alive, and very many persons perishing of hunger, especially orphan children. The brethren had always many applicants for relief in times of dearth, and nothing tended more to recommend the Gospel to the hearts and consciences of the heathen than the generous kindness they met with from their converted fellow-countrymen. By their newly-formed habits of forethought and prudent economy, the Christian Greenlanders were prepared for such seasons of distress, and they were the more frugal in supplying their own needs, that they might spare some of their stores to the destitute, hungry crowds who daily flocked to the settlement. "It is very good to be here," said one of the heathen, "because the people love one another so much." Nor was the compassionate liberality of the converts confined to their own countrymen. Nothing ever touched them more deeply than the account of the destruction which had fallen upon some of the mission settlements in America. When they heard that a party of savages had suddenly attacked one of the

stations, murdering and burning, according to
their cruel customs, and that the poor Indian
Christians who had escaped with their lives had
lost their all, the whole congregation burst into
loud weeping. " I have a fine reindeer skin to
give them," said one ; " And I have a new pair of
boots," cried another ; " And I have some oil,"
said a third, &c., &c. All contributed according
to their ability, and the money procured by the
sale of their gifts was duly forwarded to the poor
refugees in Pennsylvania.

The thoughts of Matthew Stach were still bent
towards Labrador on the one hand, and on the
other to the establishment of a mission in South
Greenland. The poverty of the Moravian community threw, indeed, many difficulties in the
way of any new undertaking ; but in faith and
prayer they had encountered many difficulties,
and overcome them, and their long-tried missionary had a good hope that in this case also the way
would be made plain before them. The mission
at New Herrnhut was well supplied with labourers, additional missionaries having come out from
Europe ; and his early companions, John Beck and
Frederic Bœhnisch, carrying on the work with
undiminished zeal, and an activity very little
impaired by years. It appeared to Matthew
Stach that the time was come when he might law-
fully hold himself in readiness for service in
another field ; and at the end of twenty-one years'
labour in Greenland, he returned to Germany to

place himself at the disposal of his brethren. Shortly before his departure, the Danes had founded another trading settlement in Fisher's Bay, a narrow fiord about thirty-six leagues southward of Godhaab. Near the mouth of the bay are two islands, from twelve to sixteen miles in circumference, on the southernmost of which the Danes had established their factory. It so happened that Matthew Stach was obliged to take shipping for Europe at this new settlement. Before embarking, he took a view of the surrounding country, amongst the inhabitants of which were many families who had occasionally spent the summer fishing season near New Herrnhut, and had become acquainted with the missionary. They prayed him that teachers might be settled in their district also, and he undertook to convey their request to his brethren in Europe. Accordingly, on arriving in Germany he laid the matter before the congregation at Herrnhut, and application was made to the Danish government for permission to found the proposed mission. It was promptly granted; but the Moravian Brethren were not able to avail themselves of it until two or three years had elapsed, during which the inhabitants of the Fisher's Fiord still urged their request for teachers as often as any of them visited the missionaries. In the year 1757, however, it was determined that Matthew Stach should undertake this new mission, planting a little Christian settlement at once, on the plan of that at New Herrn-

hut, with the help of some of the native families
from that place. Amongst the brethren in Germany who had, in heart, devoted themselves to
missionary labour was Jens **Haven,** who, like
Stach, cherished an ardent desire to proclaim the
Gospel in Labrador. But as it was not at that
time practicable to attempt anything for the
Esquimaux of that country, Jens **Haven** and his
brother Peter willingly agreed to accompany
Matthew Stach. They could make no extensive
preparations—a boat was almost the only article
of use and comfort which they carried with them.

They set out in March, 1758, crossed the
theatre of war unmolested, and proceeded to
Copenhagen; but the ship lying there bound for
Fisher's Lodge and Godhaab was already so full
that they could not get a passage on board of her,
and were obliged to wait a month till another
vessel, bound for the Danish factory at Zukkertop, one hundred leagues northward of their destination, should sail. At Zukkertop they embarked for Godhaab in their open boat, and
reached it safely on the fourth day, after a rough
passage. Their arrival caused great gladness at
New Herrnhut, where a consultation concerning
the proposed mission was quickly entered upon.
Four native families, numbering in all thirty-two
souls, were selected to be, with the missionaries,
the founders of the new settlement, for which the
whole party set sail in July. But the first care
was to explore the fiord for the most suitable spot.

The immediate neighbourhood of the Danish factory was very congenial to European tastes, being well watered, and covered with luxuriant grass. But the missionaries knew that, desirable as this spot appeared to themselves, it would be far less agreeable to the Greenlanders, because less suitable for their pursuits. And they endeavoured to find a place which should combine these two advantages—a spring which was never frozen to the bottom, and a strand which remained open in winter, and was not at too great a distance from the ocean, that the Southland Greenlanders, who were mostly accustomed to live near the open sea, might not be deterred, by the dread of starvation, from frequenting the new settlement and hearing the Gospel. No such place was to be found in the fiord, excepting Akonemiok, an island about three miles from the ocean; and though it was so closely environed with mountains that they could not catch a glimpse of the sun, the missionaries, with their usual self-denial, chose this spot for the sake of the natives. They pitched their tents there on the 24th July; and the first care of all was to erect more permanent dwellings, the missionaries contenting themselves for the present with a Greenland house, as they had no timber with which to erect one after the European fashion. So devoid was the site of building materials, that they were forced to roll the stones to the spot. bring the earth in bags from one place, and fetch

the sods by water from another. They had, however, brought some laths for the roof from New
Herrnhut, and the sea wafted to them two large
pieces of timber, such as they needed to complete
it. Besides a small apartment for domestic pur-
poses, the house contained a room fifteen feet
square, which, until they could procure a church
and school, served for both. The roof was nearly
six feet high, without ceiling, and supported by
two pillars; the laths covered with a double
layer of sods, cemented with earth to keep out
the rain, and old tent-skins being spread over
the whole; the walls also were lined with skins.

At first the Greenlanders found it difficult to
maintain themselves, but afterwards discovered,
not far from home, a strait through which the seals
ran into a narrow bay, where they might be taken
in great numbers. It was not long before some of
the heathen dwellers in the neighbourhood came
to visit the new settlers, some instigated by curiosity, but more by a desire to hear the Word of
God. Most of them lived in places which involved a journey of some miles over rugged rocks
before they could reach the mission station; yet
they came frequently, especially at Christmas,
when the Christian natives and their teachers met
more often for public worship, and celebrated
their festival with joyful hymns and anthems of
praise. The first winter was so mild that neither
storms nor ice hindered the people from going
out constantly to catch seals, &c., in the neigh-

bouring bays and creeks, by which means they procured abundance of provisions, and were not obliged to leave the station until the season for the caplin fishery arrived, and all betook themselves to the teeming seas. The missionaries who accompanied them frequently found attentive hearers amongst the heathen natives who were engaged in the same pursuit; and if the missionaries were not present, the heathen frequently invited their converted fellow-countrymen to come into their tents, and speak to them the Word of God. Nor was the simple testimony of these native Christians without effect. By it many individuals, and even large families, were induced to change their abode, and come to live near the missionaries, though the removal was, in many cases, detrimental to their temporal comfort. Other native families, stopping at the station on their migration northwards, heard the word of God, their Creator, and the tidings of redemption by the blood of Christ, for the first time, and with great astonishment, and even emotion. They could not, however, decide to stay and settle in that neighbourhood; but the missionaries were glad that they had got some intelligence of the Gospel, and knew where to seek for it when they wanted consolation.

The missionaries had named their settlement Lichtenfels, i. e., Light-rock, from the colour of the rocks which surrounded it. "No one," says the historian of the mission, " would conceive such a nook to be fit for the habitation of human beings." Nor was any abundance or variety of food to be obtained on the land, reindeer, eider-

LICHTENFELS.

fowl, &c., not frequenting the neighbourhood. But the sea yielded cod and halibut, which the natives stored for winter provision. The second winter was very long, and excessively severe. Looking from the mountain tops, towards the end of May, the sea was still ice-locked as far as the eye could reach. Both missionaries and natives were now reduced to great straits, and though not totally without food, owing to their prudent fru-

gality, they were rarely able to satisfy their
hunger. But no one complained, and each helped
the others as far as he was able. All were much
encouraged by the accession, in the course of this
year, of several heathen families, numbering in
all fifty-five souls, who came to settle at Lichtenfels, " in order," as they said, " to be converted."
In the third year from the foundation of the
settlement, the congregation consisted of one hundred and thirty-seven natives. This increase in
their numbers made the missionaries long for a
church in which their people could assemble, for
they had no place of meeting large enough, and
bad weather often prevented them from holding
their services in the open air. Their brethren in
Europe had not been unmindful of their need, and
in the summer of 1761 materials ready framed
for a church and dwelling-house reached the
mission-station. The captain of the ship which
had brought them out lent some of his men to
assist in the erection ; and when the Greenlanders
had all returned from their fishing expeditions,
and were duly settled for the winter at Lichtenfels, the church was solemnly dedicated to the
worship of God on the 1st November, being the
24th Sunday after Trinity.

After the services of the day were concluded, a
feast was held, in which all participated, and the
general spirit of cheerful thankfulness and goodwill made up for the simplicity of the fare, which
consisted chiefly of dried caplins. A hymn of

praise, composed by John Beck for this occasion, and sung with great spirit by the Greenlanders, closed the festivities. The church was larger than that at New Herrnhut. A dwelling-house of six rooms immediately adjoined it, and behind it the missionaries had industriously converted a boggy piece of ground into a garden. In front were the native houses ; on a height, at some distance, lay the place of burial. Ridges of rock rose around the station, and beyond them the wall of ice-clad mountains.

In the following year the mission at Lichtenfels being now, by the blessing of God, well-esta blished, and John Beck having come to assist Matthew Stach in the charge of the congregation, Jens Haven resigned his post. An opening appeared now to be made for commencing a mission in Labrador, and he returned to Germany that he might prepare to enter upon his long-desired field of labour. On the voyage homeward he was gratified by the unusual appearance of a rainbow which did not consist of the usual colours, but was quite white with the exception of a pale grey stripe in the middle. Shortly before the sailing of the ship from Greenland, an equally unusual but more beautiful sight had been presented to some of the brethren who were near the Kookörnen islands, in Baal's River. The islands appeared, at first, much magnified as if seen through a telescope, so that all the rocky points and chasms filled with ice, were plainly discernible.

After some time all the islets seemed connected together, and took the shape of trees; then the scene shifting once more, a charming display of ships in full sail with flying colours, mountain castles with ruined turrets, and numberless other objects, rose to view, which, after deluding the eye for a short time with their fanciful imagery, all either rose aloft, or receded in the distance till they vanished out of sight.

Until the summer of 1763, death made no breach in the band of brothers who had solemnly bound themselves, twenty-eight years before, to the service of the Gospel in Greenland; but in that year Frederic Bœhnisch rested from his labours. His course had been marked by unflagging perseverance. Watchful over everything which concerned either the temporal or spiritual interests of the people, he could hardly be prevailed upon to intermit any of his accustomed duties, even when sickness was visibly wasting his strength. The latter months of his life were greatly cheered by the presence and assistance of his son, who, having been educated in Germany, and prepared for usefulness in the mission, returned to take part in the work under the direction of his father. A severe fall from a rock hastened the dissolution of the elder Bœhnisch. Feeling that his end drew nigh, he desired that his friend Matthew Stach might be sent for. To him he bequeathed the care of the flock at New Herrnhut, until additional missionaries should arrive from Germany.

His last earthly duty being now fulfilled, and having received for the last time the Holy Communion, Frederic Bœhnisch tenderly bade farewell to his wife and children, and departed, full of hope and peace, in the fifty-fourth year of his age. He was greatly lamented by the Christian Greenlanders, and many reproached themselves, now it was too late, that they had not profited more by the instructions of one who had so assiduously cared for their souls.

In 1763, three additional missionaries arrived from Europe; and Matthew Stach, still intent on carrying the Gospel to South Greenland, proposed to explore all the coast from Lichtenfels to Cape Farewell, to discover the fittest spot for the mission settlement which he hoped to see eventually planted there, and to preach the Gospel in every place where he could find hearers. He calculated that a year or more would be thus spent; but the many dangers, foreseen and unforeseen, with which the expedition would probably be attended, made his brethren and himself feel that it was indeed uncertain whether they would ever meet again in this life. He took an affectionate leave of the congregations at New Herrnhut and Lichtenfels, and begged their prayers that the Word of God might be made known to the Southland heathen. He was accompanied by several native converts who had originally come from the South, and who hoped to find out their kindred and persuade them to listen to the glad tidings of a Redeemer.

Several months were spent in searching out the
coast; sometimes amid scenes of wild desolate
grandeur, where

> " Drear Cold for ages
> Thrones him; and, fixed on his primæval mound,
> Ruin, the giant, sits."

But the dreary aspect of wildernesses of rock and
precipice would often have made the heart of the
missionary sink, had there not been, even in these
places, many immortal souls to whom he and his
assistants joyfully made known the message of
the Gospel. The spring of 1766 found them in
the warmest and most agreeable part of Greenland, where numerous fiords wound thirty or
forty miles inland, having on their banks many
thickets and verdant spots, most refreshing to
eyes wearied with the monotony of ice and snow.
Several grassy levels showed traces of ancient cultivation, and here also were ruins of churches,
and even fragments of church bells. But the
heathen dwellers in the land had made the place
of Christian worship their cemetery, and its walls
were the quarry from whence they had taken stones
to close up the graves of their dead. Twenty
miles south of this series of fiords, lay the Eden
of Greenland, Isle Onartok (*Warmth*). Here a
warm spring, perpetually bubbling up, irrigated
with its streams a luxuriant meadow-ground, ena-
melled with many-coloured flowers. On the oppo-
site coast many hundred heathen dwelt, amongst
whom the missionary found no small number of

healers. That the seed so widely scattered in this
voyage found some hearts prepared to receive it,
appeared the next year, when many of the Southland Greenlanders repaired to Lichtenfels.

And here it may be remarked, that although the
people, in their heathen condition, generally appeared so engrossed with the cares and labours of
their hazardous mode of existence, as to have no
leisure for thought concerning things spiritual
and immortal, there were some amongst them of
a more reflective turn of mind ; men in whom
natural religion had spoken of an unknown God,
and who were ready to welcome the revelation
which He had given of Himself. A company of
baptized Greenlanders conversing together one
day, some of them expressed surprise that they
could have spent so many years of life in contented ignorance and thoughtlessness, neither
knowing whence they came, nor whither they
were going. One of the party immediately replied : " It is true that we were formerly ignorant
heathens, knowing nothing of God ; for who,"
continued he, turning to the missionaries who
were present, " could have informed us of Him
before your arrival? Yet I have often thought, a
kayak, with the darts belonging to it, does not
exist of itself; it must be made with the trouble
and skill of men's hands, and he who does not
understand the use of it quickly spoils it. Now
the least bird is made with greater art than the
best kayak, and no man can make a bird. But

man himself is yet far more artfully composed than a bird ; who then can have made *him?* Some of our people say, that the first man rose out of the earth. But I could never believe it; for if it were so, why do not men grow out of the earth now? And from whence did the earth come? and the sea, the sun, and moon? Thinking upon all these things, I became sure that there must be some One, far more mighty and skilful than man, who had made them all. Yet who has heard or seen Him? Not one of us. But I thought there might, perhaps, be, in some place, men who had seen Him, or who knew something about Him; and I wished that if there were any such, I could speak with them. As soon, therefore, as I heard you speak of this mighty Lord, I was glad, and I believed your words." Another man added : "I, too, had such thoughts ; for it seemed to me wonderful that we were so different from other creatures, that they served us for food and seemed made for our use ; and yet, although there was no creature wiser than man, we often felt afraid ; and when we thought of dying, we feared lest some evil might come upon us after death. I used to think, who can it be that we are afraid of? we see no one above us in the world. Can there be some Great One whom we do not see? Oh, if I could but know Him, and have Him for my friend !"

In July 1766, the congregation at Lichtenfels were rejoiced by the return of Matthew Stach from his exploring voyage. He was followed by some of the strangers whom his exhortations had awakened, and who now left their distant homes to join themselves to the believers. In the following year many more came to hear a repetition of the truths which the missionary had told them during his sojourn in the South. Having received permission to be present at the services of the church, they attended with remarkable diligence, and appeared to be greatly interested in them, especially in those of Passion Week and Easter. Sixty persons now joined themselves to the inhabitants of the little Christian settlement; and a still larger increase took place at New Herrnhut, where many of the natives who dwelt on the neighbouring shores and islands, and had heard the Word of God preached for years without giving serious heed to it, now awoke, as it were from slumber. Much to the surprise of the missionaries, messengers came also from a distance, sent by an Angekok, named Immenek, a man of wealth and consequence amongst his countrymen, to bring him back, as he said, " good words." He had grown gray in the practice of his art, but had not been chargeable with the grosser crimes of which many of its professors were guilty. Now, however, he was suddenly arrested in his career by an alarming anticipation of future judgment, and withdrew apart into a solitary place, where he continued for several days, none knowing what had become of him. He had formerly heard the missionaries preach, but had paid no attention to their words; but they returned in some degree to his mind now, and he came out of his retirement, resolving to take up his abode among the believers. Calling together all his family and neighbours, he confessed that he had been all his life imposing upon the credulity of his countrymen, and declared that he would do so no longer. As soon as the return of spring enabled him to remove, with his children and all that he had, he would go to New Herrnhut; meanwhile he sent three of his people to bring back, if possible, a teacher. Two of the national assistants accompanied Immenck's messengers on their return; and were overjoyed at the reception which they met with, not only from the old chief, but from all the inhabitants of his village. They were scarcely allowed time to eat or sleep, so eagerly did the people press to hear something more of God and the Saviour; and it seemed as if neither old nor young could be satisfied without being told again and again, that "great wonder," that the Almighty God came into the world to die for fallen man. On the 1st of May, a long procession of boats and kayaks was seen steering towards New Herrnhut. Immenck, his kindred, and neighbours, were all come to learn the way of life; and the population of the settlement was augmented by an accession of eighty persons. "In these," say the missionaries, " the parable of the sower and his seed was remarkably exemplilied." From the hearts of some, the evil one snatched away the seed of the Word; or the weeds of earthly care stifled its growth. Others received it with joy, but the ground was unprepared by any deep conviction of sin, and the quickly-springing plant was presently blighted by temptation. But in the hearts of Immenek and many others, the doctrine of redemption by the blood of Christ became the root whence sprang enduring fruits of righteousness.

In the year 1771 Matthew Stach closed his long and successful labours in Greenland. The infirmities of advancing age no longer permitted him to take that active part in the mission which had been his delight; and he returned to Germany, to seek a post better adapted to the feebleness of old age, yet where his remaining strength might be spent in his Master's service. In a letter addressed to him shortly before his departure, John Beck takes a grateful retrospect of the years in which they had laboured together, and of the increase which God had granted. From this letter also we learn that the large addition made of late years to the inhabitants of the mission stations was not an unmixed good. "We two," he says, "have not yet put off the house of clay from whence our beloved Frederic Bœhnisch departed, seven years ago, to the presence of Jesus. We three it was who, in the year 1735, made that solemn vow, one with another, wholly to follow our Lord in this land; to do all, and bear all, as unto Him; and for His sake, and the souls of these poor Greenlanders, not to love our lives unto the death. He graciously accepted our desire to serve Him, and in His unspeakable condescension and mercy has crowned our work with blessing. He has kept His promise, though we have often withstood Him; for which I, for my part, am truly ashamed, and do often with tears pray Him to absolve me. These congregations, which we have seen grow up from the very beginning, and to which, according to the ability given unto us, we have ministered; how far do they exceed all our early prayers, thoughts, and anticipations! How many times we besought Him, weeping, to grant us even but *one* soul out of this nation; because we knew that even one soul was more precious than all the treasures of the earth in His sight who had given His blood to redeem it. But He stayed not at *one*. Already hath He gathered into His treasure-house five hundred souls who had fled to Him for refuge; and nearly that number still dwell in the body at New Hernnhut, while here also, at Lichtenfels, are three hundred over whom His eye watches. Over these, on the whole, I cannot but rejoice, and praise Him daily for what He has done and is doing in their behalf. For truly we have, in these our congregations brethren and sisters in Christ whose heart's desire it is to serve Him. Yet while we wander here never will the wish cease to rise—Would to God ye all might live before Him! For we have now amongst us too many who have outwardly joined themselves to the believers, not knowing truly in whom they believe; and by these harm arises to the others. In our early beginnings it was not so. But now many of our people have come amongst us because their kindred were become Christians; and while they conform to the regulations of the settlement, and are not outwardly blameable in conduct, I do not see that we ought to exclude them. But I am sure that we do wrong if we hastily administer to such careless souls the blessings of the Church, and especially if we encourage them to partake of the Lord's table. For I have observed that such persons, after they have been advanced to that privilege, settle down careless and contented in their lukewarmness, saying in their hearts, ' I have attained all now; there is nothing more for me to do.' "

The two elder sons of this excellent man devoted themselves to missionary service, and for a few years laboured under his direction; at the end of that time the brethren in Europe called one of them to join the mission in Labrador. His father blessed him for the last time, and sent him away. Soon afterwards, in the year 1777, the veteran missionary fell asleep, having fulfilled forty-three years of patient, faithful labour. His last days were marked by much bodily suffering, but no cloud darkened the peace and hope which filled his mind. He had been permitted to see the foundation of a third mission-station, so long

the object of his prayers and those of his friend
Matthew Stach. It was situated on the shores of
a fiord a few miles distant from the Isle of Onartok, amidst a large heathen population, some of
whom resorted to the missionaries with readiness.
Every year saw an increase in the number of converts. This was joyful news to Matthew Stach,
who from his distant abode still looked constantly
towards the land in which he had fed his Master's
flock so many years. He had retired to one of
the American settlements of the brethren, endeared to him by the fraternal welcome extended to
himself and his Greenland converts twenty-three
years before. He occupied himself in the education of the children ; but his warmest sympathies
were with the work which was being carried on
in Greenland and Labrador. The Christians of
another race who now surrounded him shared his
affection for their Esquimaux brethren, and in
the year 1783 joyfully celebrated with him the
jubilee of the Greenland mission. Four years
afterwards Matthew Stach rested from his labours.

The first attempt at planting a mission in
Labrador was made in the year 1752, when some
London merchants assisted the brethren to fit out
a vessel for a trading voyage to the coast. Four
missionaries embarked in her, and also a Dutch-
man, named Erhard, who had lately joined the
brethren, and who, in his previous occupation as
mate of a Greenland whaling-vessel, had acquired
some knowledge of the Greenlandic or Esqui-

maux tongue. In July the ship arrived off the
Labrador coast, and anchored in a large bay,
which the missionaries named Nisbet's Haven,
after one of the owners of the vessel. Here they
resolved to settle, built a wooden house—the frame
and materials for which they had brought with
them—and, in the cheerful anticipation of future
labour, called the place Hopedale. Erhard meanwhile proceeded with the ship farther north, for
the purpose of trading with the natives. As
they were afraid, however, to visit him on board
the ship, because of the guns which she carried,
and pressed him greatly to come on shore to
them, he went in an unarmed boat, with five of
the crew, into a bay where there were numerous
islands. None of the party returned again. The
boat which they had taken was the only one the
ship possessed, and the captain, after waiting some
days, and vainly endeavouring to ascertain what
had become of them, was obliged to return to
Nisbet's Haven, and to tell the missionaries that,
having lost so many of his best men, he could not
work the ship back to Europe unless they assisted
him. They could not refuse, though they deeply
regretted to quit their work even before it was
begun. The following year the ship returned, and
the search made for Erhard and his companions re-
sulted in the melancholy discovery of their remains,
with evident marks of a violent death upon them.

This display of murderous ill-will on the part
of the Esquimaux forced the brethren to suspend.

their design of planting a mission, though it was never lost sight of. But in 1764 Jens Haven, who had recently returned from Greenland, resumed the enterprise. In England he was introduced to Sir Hugh Palliser, Governor of Newfoundland, who warmly approved of his design, and immediately on arriving in the island issued a proclamation, requiring all persons whom it might concern, to render Mr. Haven every assistance in their power. Notwithstanding the Governor's support, however, Haven had the greatest difficulty in persuading the master of any ship to land him on the coast of Labrador, so evil a character did its inhabitants bear. He landed at last in the Isle of Quirpont, off the north-east extremity of Newfoundland, and had here his first interview with the Esquimaux. "September 4," he writes in his journal, "was the happy day on which I first saw an Esquimaux arrive in the harbour. I ran to him, and addressed him in his own language, saying, 'I am your friend.' He was struck with amazement to hear a European speaking in his own tongue, but readily consented to my request that he would go back and fetch some of the chief men of his tribe, as I wished to say something to them. Meanwhile, I put on my Greenland dress, and met them on the beach, inviting them to land. 'Here is an *Innuit*' (countryman), exclaimed they, when they saw me. I said, 'I am your countryman and friend.' They were much astonished, but behaved quietly, and we continued talking for some time. Then they begged me to accompany them to an island about an hour's row from the shore, where they had left their wives and children, who would like, they said, to see me. I hesitated for a moment, for by going it was evident that I should place myself entirely in their power. But it seemed so essential to the commencement of a mission that we should treat them with confidence, and become better acquainted with the nation, that I confidently turned to the Lord in prayer, and thought, ' I will go with them in Thy name. If they kill me, my work is done, and I shall live with Thee ; but if they spare my life, I will firmly believe that it is Thy will they should hear and believe the Gospel.' I went ; and as soon as we arrived they all set up a shout, ' Our friend is come !' They almost carried me to their encampment, where I was so closely beset on all sides, I could scarcely move, each man pushing forward his family to be noticed. I prevailed with them, at last, to sit down quietly and hear what I had to say. I explained my object in coming to visit them, promising that if they were willing to be taught I would return again next summer with some of my brethren, build a house on their land, and daily discourse with them of the way to happiness and everlasting life. The next day eighteen of the men returned my visit. I took this opportunity to inform them of the friendly disposition of the British Government towards them, and promised

that no injury should be done to them if they conducted themselves peaceably; and to confirm them
in this assurance, offered them a written declaration
of Governor Palliser to the same effect; but they
shrank back, supposing this writing to be alive;
nor could I by any means persuade them to accept
of it. In the barter which they carried on with
the ship's crew, they constituted me their arbiter,
'for,' said they, 'you are our friend.'" The following year Haven returned to Labrador, accompanied by three other missionaries, one of whom
had been long resident in Greenland. They were
welcomed in a most friendly manner by the Esquimaux, who praised Haven for being true to his
promise, and repeated much of what he had told
them in the preceding summer. On this occasion
the brethren had several opportunities of addressing the natives, and preached the Gospel to large
companies, who listened, at first, with eager curiosity, but when the novelty of the subject had
worn off, their interest in it quickly subsided.
Like their kinsmen, the Greenlanders, in their
heathen state, the people of Labrador cared
nothing for a subject which did not appear calculated to assist them in their daily pursuits.
But they evinced the utmost confidence in the
goodwill of the missionaries; and the latter desired nothing more than to take up their abode
amongst them. Notwithstanding, however, the
favour with which Governor Palliser and several
persons of influence in England regarded the pro

ject of a mission, difficulties were interposed by others, which retarded the accomplishment of the plan for several years. At length, in May, 1769, an order in Council was issued, to the effect, " That the land desired in Esquimaux Bay should be granted to the Unitas Fratrum, and their Society, for the furtherance of the Gospel among the heathen, and they be protected in their laudable undertaking." Again Haven sailed for Labrador, and selected a suitable spot for the future mission settlement, considerably to the north of the harbour which had been fixed upon in 1752. He formally purchased the ground from the Esquimaux, who testified the highest gratification at the proceeding; and in the following year a company of fourteen persons, among whom were two missionaries, a surgeon, and two or three men well skilled in carpentry and smith's work, laid the foundation of the little Christian community. The place they called Nain. Some hundreds of Esquimaux spent the summer in the neighbourhood of the station, but on the approach of winter withdrew to various parts of the coast. Though they had constantly visited the settlers, and listened willingly to the discourses of the missionaries, no lasting impression appeared to have been made on their minds. But a few months afterwards the brethren were agreeably surprised by the tidings that Anauke, one of these savages, being on his death-bed, had spoken of Jesus as the Redeemer and Saviour of men, had continually prayed to Him, and departed in confident reliance on His mercy. " Be comforted," said he to his wife, who began to shriek and howl, like the rest of the heathen, at his approaching end; " I am going to the Saviour." His happy death had a favourable influence on his countrymen, who ever after spoke of him as " *The man whom the Saviour took to Himself.*"

Another instance of the effect produced by the preaching of the Gospel was still more remarkable, on account of the extreme youth of the person affected by it, and her entire isolation among the heathen during many succeeding years. Among the natives who abode for a short season near Nain were a man and his wife, with one little daughter. The child heard the missionaries speak of an Almighty Lord, who was also the Friend and Saviour of men, and she never forgot it. Her parents departed from the neighbourhood, and returned no more. They remained contented in their heathen darkness. But the little girl found a solitary place where, unknown to her parents and her companions, she could go and pour out her heart to that unseen Friend in whom she had learnt to trust, though she scarcely knew His name. The years of childhood were hardly over when she became an orphan, and was given in marriage by her kinsmen to a man of most brutal character, who had already taken two wives. The miseries of this marriage did not end with the death of her husband. By his

crimes he had wronged many, who afterwards
revenged themselves upon his helpless widow
and children. The unhappy children were so
miserably beaten that they died in consequence.
At this time of her deepest distress the poor
heart-broken mother was found by a country-
woman who had been converted, and who sympathized in her sorrow. She conducted her suffering sister to the missionaries; and now, to the
joy of her heart, the poor woman heard again,
much more at large, of the Lord and Friend who
had redeemed her. She was shortly baptized,
and her exemplary conduct recommended the
Gospel to many. She learnt quickly to read and
write, and the missionaries looked forward to her
becoming very useful as a helper among her
countrywomen. But her days on earth were
short. By this time more than one little congregation of converted natives had been formed.
The experience of a few years convinced the
missionaries that Nain was insufficient to serve
as a gathering-place for the Esquimaux dispersed
along six hundred miles of coast, and it afforded
them but scanty resources during the winter
season, when several would have been willing to
remain there. They resolved, therefore, to establish two other mission-stations, one to the north,
the other to the south. The voyage northward
was attended with disastrous consequences: the
ship was wrecked, and two of the brethren perished
in the waves. The survivors, however, set out

afresh the following year, and under the conduct of Haven began a new settlement at Okkak, one hundred and fifty miles north of Nain. A few years afterwards the third station was founded at Hopedale. In each of these places the missionaries met with many discouraging circumstances, and encountered many dangers in the prosecution of their work; but their success, though not rapid, was sufficient to animate them to perseverance. "In conclusion," says one of the annalists, from whom the preceding particulars of the Greenland and Labrador missions have been derived, "we thank God who has raised up a seed to serve Him in the deserts of the North. If the Lord of the harvest, who has sent forth His labourers, continue to crown their work with His blessing, we may indulge the joyful anticipation that on the great day when earth and sea shall render up their dead, the frozen rocks and icy sepulchres of Labrador and Greenland will yield no inconsiderable proportion of their charge to swell the choral shout which shall proclaim the finished work of the Redeemer, and the fulness of His reward for the travail of His soul."

THE END.

WYMAN AND SONS, PRINTERS, GREAT QUEEN STREET, LONDON.

PUBLICATIONS

Society for Promoting Christian Knowledge.

*Most of these Works may be had in Ornamental Bindings,
with Gilt Edges, at a small extra charge.*

Price
s. d

Africa Unveiled.
By the Rev. H. ROWLEY. With Map, and eight full-
page illustrations on toned paper. Crown 8vo. *cloth boards* 5 0

An Eventful Night, and What came of it.
Adapted from the German of Ernst Andolt. With three
page illustrations. Fcap. 8vo.................. *cloth boards* 1 0

Clary's Confirmation : a Tale for Girls.
With two full-page illustrations on toned paper.
Crown 8vo..*cloth boards* 1 6

Cringlewood Court.
By F. SCARLETT POTTER, author of "Out-of-Doors
Friends," &c. With three full-page illustrations on
toned paper. Crown 8vo....................... *cloth boards* 2 6

Drifted Away.
A Tale of Adventure. With three full-page illustrations
on toned paper. Crown 8vo....................*cloth boards* 2 6

Fifth Continent (The), with the adjacent Islands.
Being an Account of Australia, Tasmania, and New
Guinea, with Statistical Information to the latest date.
By CHARLES H. EDEN, Author of "Australia's Heroes,'
&c. With Map. Crown 8vo................. *cloth boards* 5 0

For Faith and Fatherland.
By M. BRAMSTON, Author of "Rosamond Ferrars,"
&c. With three full-page illustrations on toned paper.
Crown 8vo.. *cloth boards* 2 6

Girls of Bredon (The); and Manor House Stories.
By Mrs. STANLEY LEATHES. With three full-page
illustrations on toned paper. Crown 8vo... *cloth boards* 2 0

**Great Captain (The) : An eventful Chapter in
Spanish History.**
By ULICK R. BURKE, M.A. With two full-page illus-
trations on toned paper. Crown 8vo..........*cloth boards* 2 0

1-5-79.]   [12mo. or fcap. 8vo.

Harry Preston; or, "To him that overcometh."
A Story for Boys. By the Author of "Ellen Mansel."
With three full-page illustrations on toned paper.
Crown 8vo...*cloth boards* 1 6

Harvey Compton's Holiday.
By the Author of "Percy Trevor's Training," "Two
Voyages," &c. With three full-page illustrations on
toned paper. Crown 8vo........................ *cloth boards* 1 6

Heroes of the Arctic and their Adventures.
By FREDERICK WHYMPER, Esq., author of "Travels
in Alaska." With Map, eight full-page illustrations and
numerous small woodcuts. Crown 8vo...... *cloth boards* 5 0

Hidden Workings.
By Miss H. R. RUSSELL, author of "Muriel," &c.
With three full-page illustrations on toned paper.
Crown 8vo...*cloth boards* 2 0

**In and Out of London; or, the Half-Holidays of a
Town Clerk.**
By the Rev. W. J. LOFTIE, B.A., author of "A Century
of Bibles," &c. With four full-page illustrations and
numerous small engravings. Post 8vo....... *cloth boards* 2 6

In the Marsh.
By Miss B. C. CURTEIS. With three full-page illustrations on toned paper. Crown 8vo..........*cloth boards* 2 6

King's Warrant (The).
A Tale of Old and New France. By A. H. ENGEL-
BACH, author of "Lionel's Revenge," &c. With three
full-page illustrations on toned paper. Crown 8vo.
cloth boards 2 6

Kitty Bligh's Birthday.
By ALFRED H. ENGELBACH, Esq., author of "Lionel's
Revenge," &c. With three full-page illustrations on
toned paper. Crown 8vo. ....*cloth boards* 1 6

Left in Charge.
Being the History of My Great Responsibility. By
AUSTIN CLARE, author of "The Carved Cartoon,"
&c. With three full-page illustrations on toned paper.
Crown 8vo...*cloth boards* 1 6

Little Brown Girl (The).
A Story for Children. With three full-page illustrations
on toned paper. Crown 8vo. ....*cloth boards* 2 6

Price.
s. d.

London Sparrows.
By the Author of "Ruth Lee," &c. With three full-page illustrations on toned paper. Crown 8vo. *cloth boards* 1 6

Mate of the "Lily" (The); or, Notes from Harry Musgrave's Log Book.
By W. H. G. KINGSTON, author of "Owen Hartley," &c. With three full-page Illustrations on toned paper. Crown 8vo. .... *cloth boards* 1 6

Ned Garth; or, Made Prisoner in Africa.
A Tale of the Slave Trade. By W. H. G. KINGSTON, author of "Owen Hartley," "Two Shipmates," &c. With three full-page illustrations on toned paper. Crown 8vo. .... *cloth boards* 2 6

North Wind and Sunshine.
By ANNETTE LYSTER. With three full-page illustrations on toned paper. Crown 8vo.........*cloth boards* 2 6

Our Valley.
By the Author of "The Children of Seeligsberg," &c. With three full-page illustrations on toned paper. Crown 8vo. .... *cloth boards* 2 6

Owen Hartley; or, Ups and Downs.
A Tale of the Land and Sea. By William H. G. KINGSTON, Esq. With five full-page illustrations on toned paper. Crown 8vo.........................*cloth boards* 2 6

Percy Trevor's Training.
By the Author of "Two Voyages," &c. With three full-page illustrations on toned paper. Crown 8vo. *cloth boards* 2 6

Rosebuds.
By the Author of "Our Valley," &c. With three full-page illustrations on toned paper. Crown 8vo. *cloth boards* 2 6

Royal Banner (The):
A Tale of Life Before and After Confirmation. By AUSTIN CLARE, author of "The Carved Cartoon," &c. With three full-page illustrations on toned paper. Crown 8vo. .... *cloth boards* 2 6

Seppi.
Adapted from the German of Franz Hoffmann. By M. MONTGOMERY CAMPBELL. With three page illustrations. Fcap. 8vo. .... *cloth boards* 1 6

Price.
s. d.

Shepherd of Ardmuir (The).

By Miss A. C. CHAMBERS. With three full-page illustrations on toned paper. Crown 8vo......... *cloth boards*   2   6

Silent Jim: a Cornish Story.

By JAMES F. COBB, Esq., Author of "A Tale of Two Brothers," &c. With four full-page illustrations on toned paper. Crown 8vo........................ *cloth boards*   3   6

Snowball Society (The): a Story for Children.

By M. BRAMSTON, Author of "Rosamond Ferrars," &c. &c. With three full-page illustrations on toned paper. Crown 8vo.................................*cloth boards*   2   6

Snow Fort and the Frozen Lake (The); or, Christmas Holidays at Pond House.

By EADGYTH. With three full-page illustrations on toned paper. Crown 8vo........................ *cloth boards*   2   6

Stories from Italian History.

By B. MONTGOMERIE RANKING. With two full-page illustrations on toned paper. Crown 8vo.... *cloth boards*   1   6

Two Musicians.

Tales for My Young People. By Franz Hoffmann. Translated and arranged by M. MONTGOMERY CAMPBELL. With three page illustrations. Fcap. 8vo... *cloth boards*   1   6

Two Voyages, and What came of Them.

By the Author of "A Child of the Glens," "Motherless Maggie," &c. With three full-page illustrations on toned paper. Crown 8vo.................................. *cloth boards*   2   0

Walter Campbell; or, The Chorister's Reward.

By the Author of "Ellen Mansel," &c. With three page illustrations. 18mo. ....*cloth boards*   1   0

Wilford Family (The); or, Hero Worship in the Schoolroom.

By EADGYTH. With three full-page illustrations on toned paper. Crown 8vo ....*cloth boards*   1   6

Depositories :

NORTHUMBERLAND AVENUE, CHARING CROSS;

43, QUEEN VICTORIA STREET; 48, PICCADILLY;

AND BY ALL BOOKSELLERS.

www.ingramcontent.com/pod-product-compliance
Lightning Source LLC
Chambersburg PA
CBHW030111030726
47498CB00007B/2344